The Girls

The Girls

A story of village life

by John Bowen

HAMISH HAMILTON: LONDON

First published in Great Britain 1986
by Hamish Hamilton Ltd
Garden House 57–59 Long Acre London WC2E 9JZ

Copyright © 1986 by John Bowen

British Library Cataloguing in Publication Data

Bowen, John, *1924–*
   The girls: a story of village life.
   I. Title
   823′.914[F]   PR6052.O85

   ISBN 0–241–11867–0

Phototypeset by Input Typesetting Ltd, London
Printed in Great Britain by
Billing and Sons Ltd, Worcester

CONTENTS

For Frank Kermode

FOREWORD

For the geography of the village in this story I have used (not very exactly) the village of Tysoe near which I myself live, and I have used my own house on the hill above Tysoe as a basis for the girls' house, but the characters of the story have all, with one exception, been invented. Only Mrs Marshall has been taken from life. The real Mrs Marshall died in 1982, mourned by many in the village, not least by me.

As always I have relied heavily on others for information and advice. My thanks are due and gratefully offered to Dr Peter Acland for pathology and Martin Bailey for pigs, to Amanda Evans and Louise Giblin who run the Craft Factory in the village but do not in any other way resemble the girls, to Dr Greenway for obstetrics, to Andy Armitage and Mike Foxwell who showed me how to make goats' milk cheese, to Maureen Duffy, David Cook, Patrick Woodcock, Elaine Greene, Roger and Nicola Gregory, Lillian Hopkins, Ralph Marshall and Margaret Marshall, Robert and Iestyn Tronson, and to Mr Hayward of Stratford-upon-Avon R.D.C., an expert on septic tanks.

THE SEPTIC TANK

The septic tank is in the shrubbery at the bottom of the garden. It is covered with concrete slabs, over which cotoneaster has been trained. The shrubs of the shrubbery surround it, and, one must assume, feed off its contents, the roots of berberis and buddleia, of mock-orange, dogwood, potentilla and rugosa pushing in a tangle through the brickwork. As the bricks have been pushed aside, the nourishing seepage has permeated the whole shrubbery, brightening the yellow of forsythia and the poisonous laburnum, and reaching even the Siberian crab on the corner, which produces every spring blossom as pink and bountiful as the hair of a romantic novelist, and every autumn a weight of bright red crab apples only a small proportion of which can be turned into jelly, leaving the remainder, until they drop in March, to sustain half the squirrels of the West Midlands through even the bleakest winter. Only in summer, and particularly when the wind blows from the south-west across the lawn, the septic tank gives out a strong stench, and guests move uneasily a little nearer the house. 'Oh, it is a body,' the girls say. 'We have a body in there, no one you know. It decomposes, of course, but so slowly one quite despairs.' Although the girls have lived for nearly twenty years in their cottage, the Council has never been required to empty the septic tank. There are said to be bacteria in it which eat up faeces, and are quite unaffected by detergent in the washing-up water, Beauty Without Cruelty sham-

1

poos in the bath water, and even the household bleach which is used to clean the bowl of the w.c.

The girls. Miss Hallas and Miss Burt, Janet and Susan, Jan and Sue.

THE DAY THE PIG ESCAPED

It was a day in summer when the pig escaped, the time not long past twelve and a real scorcher. Janet had opened the shop-door to let in a breeze, but there was no breeze nor any prospect of customers unless someone should come in for Elderflower Cooler or home-made ginger beer. The Elderflower Cooler, made with honey and lemon juice as well as elderflower water, was particularly refreshing and a new line, but its sale had so far been disappointing; the village children and their mothers preferred Coke and Pepsi from the Spar. However, it did not go off, or not for some days when kept in the Cold Cabinet, and any passing trade which might stop would probably come back for more; it was so very delicious.

Most people laid most of the blame for the escape and its consequences on Tatty Wakeham, a local layabout who lived off his allotment, his ferrets, a few beasts kept at the bottom of his garden, and what was said to be a trade in retreaded motor tyres. It was Tatty's custom, when not otherwise engaged, to ride his motorcycle round the village with a pig across the handlebars. Well, the pig was not actually across the handlebars; pigs are too large for that. In fact, its rump rested on Tatty's lap, and its snout, ears and front legs protruded over the handlebars of the motorcycle like the figurehead of a man-of-war. Usually Tatty's collie dog sat in a basket at the back; it was typical of the man to go ferreting with a collie instead of terriers. The pig was a pet, accustomed to such a mode of travel, and never gave trouble. It had once appeared in a television adaptation of *Middlemarch*, filmed locally by the B.B.C., when it had waltzed with Tatty on its hind legs round a bonfire over which one of its cousins was later roasted whole.

It was not Tatty's pig which escaped. That would have been of no consequence, since it was tame and would come to a whistle. No, the troublesome animal was the property of a breeder from Hereford, who was taking his pedigree boar to Mr Wharton of Lower Beck to service a sow in season. Mr Wharton had a boar of his own, of course, but was worried that the bloodline of his own herd might be growing thin. The Hereford herd was notorious for vigour.

The breeder had travelled from Hereford in a Landrover with the boar in a trailer behind, a two-wheeled vehicle with high sides and a curved canvas top. At the back was a flap as high as the sides, which let down to become a ramp and was secured by ring-bolts. Loading the trailer required the most delicate judgement, since a valuable pedigree boar of guaranteed fertility and uncertain temper may not be commanded; it must be coaxed, manoeuvred by sheets of corrugated iron pressed gently against its flank, converting only at the end into a corridor leading to the ramp, up which the boar must then consent to trot as one crossing the drawbridge into a surrendered castle, after which (such treacheries are common in the animal kingdom) the ramp becomes a flap again, and is slammed quickly shut and secured by the ring-bolts. The operation requires two men, the breeder and his nephew in this case, and both were in the front seats of the Landrover on this sweaty summer day. The two corrugated iron sheets were in the back, since the boar would have to be reconfined after performing his service.

If they had gone straight to Lower Beck Farm, Mr Wharton would have offered them refreshment; he is an open-handed man, known for it, unlike some. But they were thirsty and a little uncertain of the final stage of their way. Their route ran through the village, and there on

4

the left was the pub, *The Deep Content*, Authentic Ales, with a sign outside, 'Bar Snacks. Ploughman's Lunch. Quiches. Scampi in the Basket.' There would be plenty of time. The act is soon completed once contact has been achieved. It is the achievement of contact which may require assistance – front legs guided into place, the application of vaseline; it is no wonder that there is a growing demand among pig-breeders for artificial insemination, though the pigs themselves do not complain.

It was a hot day. They saw the sign. They parked the Landrover and trailer outside *The Deep Content*, and went inside for scampi and authentic ales. While they were in the Saloon Bar, Tatty Wakeham passed slowly by on his motorcycle with his pet sow across the handlebars, and stopped to inspect the trailer. Nobody knows how the ring-bolts became unfastened.

When the ramp hit the ground, Tatty accelerated. The sow squealed. She may have had some notion of improving her bloodline, but Tatty never gave her the chance. It had been a bumpy ride from Hereford over twisting roads. The boar emerged from the trailer in a state of generalised rage. By great good fortune no dog was tied up outside the Spar, and it has been at least fifty years since small children played on village greens. The boar looked around, head lowered, and then for want of anything better to do began to move up the road in the direction taken by the sow on the motorbike.

Mrs Marshall, whose day it was for cleaning the chapel, emerged by way of the porch to shake a duster in the open air. She saw the boar, and went back indoors where Mrs Gaines was renewing the water in the altar vases, disordering the arrangement of the flowers as she did so. Mrs Marshall's flower-arrangements were much admired in the village, not least by Mrs Marshall herself, and had won prizes at Flower Shows ten miles away. However, there was nothing that a little tactful rearrangement would not remedy when Mrs Gaines had gone.

'There's a pig in the road.'

'There can't be.'

5

'If there's not, I'm a liar.'

Mrs Marshall never lied. There was a pig in the road. 'There should be someone looking after it.'

'There isn't.'

The two women returned to the porch. The boar had found in the gutter a discarded bag still containing a few crisps, and had paused to investigate it.

'That's never a Wharton pig.' They knew it could not be Tatty's, since its sex was unmistakeable, and anyway Tatty's pig was never seen in the village except on the motorbike.

'It's come out of that trailer.' Mrs Marshall raised her voice. 'Billy!' Billy wandered blinking out of the gloom of the village garage next door, where he had been servicing the doctor's car. 'Whose is that pig come out of the trailer?' The boar deposited a series of florets onto the remains of the crisp-bag. 'Dirty object!'

'Must be in the pub.'

'Go and get them out. We don't want pig-shit all over the village.'

The village green is no more than a strip of grass separating the chapel, garage, three cottages and the Gift Shop from the road, on the other side of which are the sub-post-office, the Spar and *The Deep Content*. The sub-post-office also sells drapery and simple stationery, and is the agent for a dry-cleaner. As for the Gift Shop, the girls had not known what else to call it; its stock was so diverse, and much of it could as well be given as gifts as bought for oneself.

Billy crossed the green quickly and the road slowly, watched by the boar on which he was careful not to turn his back. As he passed the trailer, the boar lifted one hoof and stamped it on the road. Billy went swiftly into the Saloon Bar.

'Is that your pig outside?'

'What?'

'Pig.'

'Where?'

'Outside.'

'Christ! Martin!' The nephew had dipped one of his scampi (bought ready-battered and frozen, and heated up in the micro-wave) into ketchup and was loth to leave it, but he pushed back his chair and stood up. 'Loose, is he?'

'In the road.'

'Martin!' The nephew left the Saloon Bar. Ketchup was like a wound on his chin.

'Stamped his feet at me.'

'Loose, loose? How'd he get loose? How'd that boar get loose? Bloody seven hundred quid, that animal! My God! Bloody seven hundred quid on the hoof, trotting up the road to Stratford!'

'Isn't he insured?'

'Not third party.' There was a dog barking out in the road, obviously a small dog, since the sound was more a yap than a bark. The breeder downed his authentic ale, grabbed a handful of French fries from the basket, and lumbered towards the door. From outside there was the sound of a woman screaming and Martin's worried voice requesting her not to panic.

Safely from the chapel porch, like privileged spectators in a box at Astley's, Mrs Marshall and Mrs Gaines had watched the whole encounter. First the stamping of the boar, and Billy's hasty disappearance into the Saloon Bar of *The Deep Content*. Then the arrival from around the corner of the pub of a small dachshund, followed by its owner, a person in pink jeans. A villager's dog would have been kept on the lead in the main street, but the pink-jeaned person was a newcomer, the merest overspill from Stratford, who had been evacuated with others from condemned property into new council houses. The intention of the Warwickshire County Council had been to reinvigorate decaying rural communities with a transfusion of new blood, but the villagers had produced antibodies to the transfusion. This pink-jeaned woman was not a chapel-goer, and it was believed that her son, among others, had vandalised the public telephone box. A dachshund! Village dogs were Jack Russells, collies, Alsatians. Mrs Marshall and Mrs Gaines had watched with approval

7

as the dachshund, possibly believing from the length of its back that the boar was a larger specimen of its own kind, had made its approach. The boar had lowered its head, made a small run towards the dachshund, and waited. Only a really stupid dog could have construed this as playful behaviour, but none of the newcomers was noted for intelligence. The dachshund, which had made a curving run, tail waving, away from the boar as it had advanced, had then returned, yapping joyfully. Martin had emerged from the Saloon Bar, said to the woman in pink jeans, 'Better not let him get too near,' and gone to the Landrover for corrugated iron.

Deep in the boar's race-memory was the knowledge of what one does when attacked by dogs. In Hereford as in Hindustan, that knowledge persists; it transcends time, defies domestication. First the dogs, then the men with spears. The dogs must be impaled on tusks, and tossed away like the rubbish they are, to lie broken at a distance while the boar makes his charge at the men. The boar lowered his head again as the dachshund approached, then lunged swiftly forwards, reaching outwards and upwards. But race-memory betrays us all. The boar had no tusks. It lifted the dachshund on its snout, and tossed it backwards, snorting. The woman in pink jeans screamed, while Martin attempted to calm her, although impeded by the corrugated iron which had become snagged in the back of the Landrover. In the chapel porch Mrs Marshall thanked God silently for the infinite bounty and variety of His judgements upon the unbeliever. Tossed high over the boar's head, the dachshund did not lie broken at a distance, but descended, yapping fearfully and claws extended, onto the boar's rump, just as the breeder, head down and arms waving, came at his lumbering run from *The Deep Content* and fell over the sheet of corrugated iron which Martin had managed to extract from the Landrover. The boar panicked, and ran from man and dog and corrugated iron over the road, across the green and through the open door of the Gift Shop.

Events which take time to tell may take very little time to happen. From the first scream of the pink-jeaned woman to the moment when the boar, its rump lacerated by the claws of a terrified dachshund, started across the road no more than twenty seconds passed. Janet had been in the back room when she heard the scream, and by the time she had emerged from it and gone to the shop-window to see what was going on, the boar was already crossing the green. It never occurred to her that a pig could be passing trade. The animal had already entered the shop before she realised what it was about.

To Martin and the breeder across the road, picking each other up amidst corrugated iron, it seemed simply that the boar had disappeared. The breeder had cut his knee – grazed it– bruised it – something, he was certain. What had Martin thought he was doing with the corrugated iron, and where was the bloody pig? The pink-jeaned woman wept noisily. She had attempted to clutch the dachshund to her bosom, partly for its protection and partly to console it. It had snapped at her, bitten right through her blouse and torn her bra. She might have lost a nipple; the dog would have to go. She had no idea where the pig was, and wouldn't tell if she knew.

But the spectators in the chapel porch knew what was what. 'It's in the shop,' Mrs Marshall shouted, and began to run. Mrs Marshall cleaned at the shop and also at the girls' cottage; she felt a responsibility. The breeder, clutching his knee, turned to look at the door of the Spar, which was closed and from behind which could be heard no commotion, and nothing untoward seen but the squashed nose of a small girl looking through. 'The shop, you bloody fool! The Gift Shop! Over here!' Mrs Marshall had become breathless, and had to stop to collect it. It was her breath (or the lack of it) which was to kill her five years later; she is still much missed in the village. Mrs Gaines had gone back inside the chapel to put a shine on the communion rail. Mrs Gaines is with us still.

Janet was not afraid, since in her experience domestic animals were not dangerous. The boar was only a pig to

9

her, and provided that she did nothing to aggravate it, would probably return the way it had come to the people who owned it and really ought to have it under rather better control. If not, it would have to be persuaded, either by herself or them. She would allow it a moment or so, and then, if it had not gone by itself or been reclaimed by its owners, she would turn it out.

The boar had paused to consider his position. He was not sure where he was or why he had come, but it seemed a quiet place, and out of the sun. Perhaps, if one waited, there would be food. A little to his right, standing stock still, there was a human being, but it gave off no smell of fear, nor it did seem to be aggressive, so it might as well be ignored.

In front of the boar was a glass display-cabinet, with a thick top of polished wood which acted as a counter. On it was the till, a paperbacked novel and a pair of spectacles, behind it a wooden rocking chair with a cushion. On glass shelves within the case were pieces of old lace and Staffordshire pottery (top shelf) and on the lower shelves pairs of handmade wooden clogs in various sizes, some for adults and some for children, and in various colours – burgundy, navy, emerald and buttercup. On wooden shelving behind the counter and along the wall on one side of it were bottles of homemade jams, jellies and chutneys, home-produced honey (some of it still in the comb), gooseberries and boysenberries in syrup, and gaily decorated boxes of homemade fudge and treacle toffee. To the other side of the counter was the door to the back room and then the cold cabinet, with milk and buttermilk, yoghurt, butter and low-fat cheese, all from goats, home-made potted meats, *confits* and pâtés, the Elderflower Cooler and the ginger beer. In front of the cold cabinet, almost an extension to it, there was a chest-freezer with salsify, ratatouille, peperonata, purées of parsnips with cream and walnuts, fruit shortcake and various made dishes and beside that was a small wooden table on which were homemade breads, a basket of eggs and small round hard cheeses of goats' milk, wrapped in vine-leaves. On the wall of the side-window there was a rack on which were hung genuine country smocks, intricately hand-stitched, of various sizes and colours, mostly shades of porridge, and there were more smocks in the front window, and more clogs and a few hand-thrown pots of great beauty on sale or return from a potter in Winchelsea.

The shop was a work of art; it had little to do with commerce. It did not pay its way, not even halfway. It is even possible, when one considers Janet's haphazard system of accounting and Susan's devotion to Irish Moss Peat in the vegetable garden, that some of the stock was sold for less than it cost to produce. Idiosyncratic, personal, less than a gallery but far more than a Gift Shop, it displayed those qualities to which the Women's Institute Markets held on Saturday mornings in country towns may aspire but seldom reach. It expressed the girls, Miss Hallas and Miss Burt, their joint personality, their world-view, the lace and the Staffordshire figures bought by them at sales, the yoghurt, the butter, the jams, *confits*, the bread all made by them, the honey from their bees, the eggs from their chickens, the vine-leaves in which the hard round cheeses were wrapped from their vine, the clogs put together by them, the smocks stitched by them, even the Winchelsea potter had been Miss Burt's Art Teacher at school and had inspired in her the most earth-moving crush. Once the shop had been the village Fire Station, converted from an old barn in the days when the fire engine had been pulled by horses. In the late nineteen fifties, which were then called 'the age of technology', the County Council had disapproved of a Fire Station with a thatched roof, and had first tried to abolish it, and then reluctantly built a new one further up the road, and the old building had fallen into neglect until reconverted by the girls.

It was unique, a work of art, and there was a pig in it.

The shop contained one imperfection, the flaw in the carpet. The girls had told each other that customers would wish to try on the hand-stitched smocks, and would require a mirror. They had provided one, but to please

11

themselves; it was not a mirror before which any customer would expect to try on a smock or any other article of clothing; it was decorative, not for use, an antique marbled mirror from Zarach, very beautiful and very expensive. It stood in the corner between the rack of smocks and the table of hard round cheeses. The boar turned his head. He could see in the antique marbled mirror an antique marbled boar, glaring at him, and from behind there came the confused noise of approaching humans. The boar charged.

Over went the table, and the hard round goats' milk cheeses bounced about the floor, shedding vine-leaves. *Smash*! went the mirror, and smash in a much smaller figure went the eggs from the basket. 'Oh God!' said Mrs Marshall, breathless, arriving at the open door, 'Oh God, save us and preserve us.' (She blamed the pink-jeaned woman for exciting the animal.) The pieces of antique marbled mirror-glass having only the corner behind them and nowhere else to go, fell forwards, so that the boar suffered primary injuries from the impact and secondary from the shards of glass falling like daggers onto his back and brow. He squealed, and ran sideways into the rack of smocks, which fell on him. 'Come out, come out of there!' Janet shouted. 'Get him out.' She took clogs from the window and threw them. The tangle of boar and rack and smocks boiled like a whirlpool. 'He's bleeding, the bugger!' Janet cried. The boar's rump appeared for a moment from the heaving porridge, and she scored a hit with a man's clog in navy. Mrs Marshall, who was a big-boned woman, taller than most men, advanced upon the tangle, and seemed about to hurl herself on it, as in the nineteen thirties the children of harvesters would fall upon rabbits as they broke from the wheat. 'Don't! The wire!' – she would be impaled on coat-hangers; she recoiled in time. Blinded by smocking, the boar broke from the rack and cannoned off the chest-freezer, knocking over the cold cabinet. Elderflower Cooler mingled with the blood on his back, and the lemon juice must have stung his wounds, for he squealed again and continued to do so. Martin and the breeder appeared with corrugated iron. 'You keep that bloody iron out of this shop,' Janet shouted. She imagined, as in some comedy routine, the two men knocking each other over with sheets of corrugated iron, while the boar ran to and fro between their feet and the contents of the shop were destroyed. She must save the display counter and its contents of Staffordshire pottery and lace. She grabbed a smock, ran round the boar, and together, one on each side, she and Mrs Marshall pushed the boar towards the door. Only one box of honey-in-the-comb fell from the shelves, and he ate that in passing.

Once out of the door, habit and custom prevailed. Calm returned. The homely touch of corrugated iron seemed to reassure the boar, and he allowed himself to be steered back across the road and into the trailer, once more to be secured by ring-bolts. The breeder left Martin with him, and returned to the shop. He looked at the shards of glass, the bloodied smocks, the tangle of wire, the yoghurt and buttermilk splashed about the floor. 'Seven hundred pound, that boar,' he said apologetically. 'Valuable animal!' 'Seven hundred pound that mirror,' said Janet. 'And you're paying for it. We're not insured against pigs.'

The breeder agreed that he was liable and would have to pay. A note would be made of the damage. A bill would be sent. He gave Janet his card, and drove on to Mr Wharton's farm where, to nobody's surprise, the boar failed to come up to scratch. But it was not the money, as Janet said first to Mrs Marshall and later to Susan. Those smocks had been hand-stitched. Soak them as long as you like and wash them in the most lukewarm water with the gentlest suds, they could not be sold as new; the work was wasted. Money would not compensate for that waste, and money would not reconstitute the mirror, which had been of a special shade of smoky lavender; she did not even know if Zarach still sold such mirrors. Every item of stock in the girls' shop had been produced (or chosen) and offered to the world with love; every item represented a portion of their lives, which were not

13

infinite; money could not replace that. Perhaps, Janet said, she was putting it a bit strongly, but that was how she felt, and Susan agreed in her no-nonsense way, 'Of course it's that. It's *exactly* that,' and Mrs Marshall also agreed, adding nevertheless her opinion that it's all swings and roundabouts in this world, and she wouldn't be surprised if takings were not considerably up in the next couple of weeks, because most of the village would be in to see what damage the pig had done.

It was a day in summer when the pig escaped. There were so many days of summer then.

3

THE SEVEN-YEAR ITCH

'Every item of stock offered to the world with love,' Jan had said, and Sue had agreed. '*Exactly* that.' "Love" is a dangerous word to use. It cannot be spoken without bringing its reality into doubt. Lovers even at the height of passion often find it hard to say, 'I love you.' The words come more easily when passion has cooled and contracted and other interests have begun to fill the space. 'I love you. Don't wait up.' – it need not be another woman; it could be the Angling Club's A.G.M. Love, once it dares to speak its name, is so easy to confuse with guilt, when 'I love you' is likely to mean 'I wish I loved you more than I do' or 'I'm used to you' or even 'Why do you continue to make emotional demands?'

'Offered to the world with love' – the work in the dairy, the work in the garden, with the bees and the chickens, the fashioning of clogs and smocks, was all this really an expression of love? For whom? For the *public*, for passing trade, for people touring the Cotswolds by car who might stop for a moment outside the shop and come in to buy? Well, no, of course not; the production and offering of these objects was an expression of the girls' love for each other, as the communal work of nuns is a public witness to their personal devotion to God: '*Who sweeps a room as for Thy laws, Makes that and the action fine.*'

Are you convinced or does it begin, once stated so, to fall to pieces? Would it not be more true to say that the shop and all the activities which supported it were habit, a means by which the girls could continue to share an occupation which necessarily involved them both, a reason, in the world's eyes and their own, to stay together? That is not ignoble. Most marriages have to fashion a structure which will allow them to persist. Even the brides of Christ wear habits. Habit is the cement which binds relationships together, but like cement it may crumble.

Sue began to ask herself the questions, 'What am I doing?', 'Where am I going?'

She was ten years younger than Jan. It is probable that she would have begun to ask these questions anyway, and that the escape of the pig with the consequent breakage of the mirror and destruction of stock was only the precipitating agent which caused the questions to be asked that summer instead of the following spring.

'What am I doing?' She was making a life; she and Jan were making a life together, and the worth of that shared life was greater than the worth of two separate lives would have been. If one didn't believe that, one might as well give up. But did she believe that? Of course she did. Sue had seen, even at the age of twenty-seven, too many lonely desperate people, achieving nothing, giving nothing, sharing nothing. She and Jan, they made a whole which was greater than the sum of its parts. 'What am I doing?' – she could make a catalogue of what she was doing, all that joyful occupation in dairy, still-room and kitchen, the planting, fertilising and harvesting, the hoeing between the rows, the application of glyphosphate to bindweed and couch, the tending of bees and chickens, the toil at needle and at last, the travelling together to Craft Fairs to set up their stall; it would fill a notebook, what she and Jan were doing. Yet, if one wanted to put it like that (and she didn't, but something now perversely seemed to make her put it like that) wasn't all this catalogue merely a list of ways to get through time, even in bed at night, even the snuggling together, the warmth and comfort of the two of them in bed at night, even that a way of passing time, of getting through life, no more?

16

'What am I doing?' '*A way of killing time for those who like time dead*' – the words rang in her head like the tolling of a bell. '*Do not send to ask for whom the bell tolls.*' Do not send to ask. Don't ask.

'Where am I going?' She was going nowhere; it would always be like this, except that they would both grow older. They were a refuge for each other, she and Janet; that was it. Their whole life was no more than a retreat from life. They had made a Wendy House together, and hid in it. It was the Forest of bloody Arden, their life together; it wasn't real.

Thus Susan, discontented at the age of twenty-seven. At nineteen, the refuge Janet offered had not been unwelcome to her.

The occasion of their first meeting had been romantic. Susan had been a student at a residential Teachers' Training College near Abingdon. Each summer term of their three-year course, the students would be variously attached to local schools for teaching practice. 'Local' in Oxfordshire can mean a distance of fifteen miles; if there should be a convenient train-service, it can mean more. In her second year Susan had been attached to a Comprehensive School at King's Sutton. She would cycle to Radley, leave her bicycle at the station, and catch the stopping train via Oxford. It made a long day, but the days of some of the other students of her year were longer.

The second year at a Teachers' Training College (though Susan did not know this, and certainly nobody told her) is the year for character-building attachments, the year when the weak break. Susan was given a class of fifteen-year-olds, low in attainment, high in resentment. Most people had given up on them, even their parents. These children had already made the discovery that their present contained no future. Some absented themselves from school, and Susan would have been grateful to them for doing so, but was required by the system to report their absence, so that they blamed her when they were forced to return. The expression of their blame, however, was

17

not much different from the conduct of those who did attend, and consisted partly of ignoring her (noisy conversation, passing of notes, reading of comics, eating, moving at will about the classroom, simulated and actual masturbation), partly of what is called 'playing her up' (banging of desk lids, cheek, asking of embarrassing personal questions, writing obscene graffiti on blackboards) and partly by a total refusal to learn anything at all from her or anyone else. She had feared and hated them, and they had known it.

It was so unfair. Susan would never, once she had her diploma, be required to teach such children, would never apply for such a job. The teaching-practice was a practice for nothing; it did no good to her or them; she was suffering for nothing. Teaching was not a vocation for Susan. She had never had any clear notion of what, when she was put to it, she would do by way of making a living; like many of us, she would have preferred childhood to go on for ever. She was not academically accomplished enough for university, so the Careers Mistress at Winchelsea had encouraged her to teach. And she had welcomed that encouragement, had wanted to teach; she really had – *little* children, or at least well-behaved children, or even handicapped children; she would really have enjoyed teaching handicapped children, provided that their handicaps were not too gross. It was so unfair.

So it happened that, on a Tuesday evening in May, sitting alone in a no-smoking compartment of a stopping train without a corridor, the unfairness of it all, the knowledge that she would have to go back on the next day, and the day after, and the day after that, and on and on, five days a week for five weeks more, and that she dared not refuse to go, that she had begun to shake in the classroom and could not keep her voice steady or meet the eyes of the regular teachers in the Staff Room, that she had a headache and it would get worse through the week, it had all come over her so strongly that she had begun to cry and could not stop. She had sat there, scrunched into a corner, dripping tears down her blouse as the

18

train had chuntered along by the canal and the chequered fields, and when the train had stopped at Tackley another passenger had joined her in the compartment, and still she had not been able to stop weeping. She had looked up, red-eyed and redder-nosed, and had said, 'I'm sorry, I'm very sorry,' and the other passenger, Janet, had pulled down the blinds on the platform-side of the compartment, sat down next to Susan, and had cuddled her. Everything had gone on from there.

Susan achieved her diploma, but never taught. Janet gave up her job with the Probation Service. Do you wish to know what happened about King's Sutton? Encouraged by Janet, Susan refused to go back, and the College approved her decision. No trainee had ever lasted a full term at King's Sutton. Its buildings were later turned into a Detention Centre for juvenile delinquents.

The girls were an old-fashioned couple, as they still are. They had come together in the days when the Women's Movement was at its most militant, and many a wife and mother was led into lesbianism by having her consciousness raised, but Susan had never heard of the Women's Movement and Janet was not sure that she approved of what she had heard. Instead they fell innocently in love, meeting at first as they could, mostly in Oxford, making excursions to Historic Homes, spending evenings together at the cinema or at undergraduate productions of obscure Jacobean plays and Sunday afternoons in physical discovery on the sofa of Janet's digs in Iffley. By the end of Susan's time at the Teachers' Training College, they had known that they wished to be left alone in each other's company, and looked for somewhere that could happen. Janet had money, a regular income from a family brewery in Cheshire, but they had needed a project also, and at first it had been self-sufficiency, and from a surplus of self-sufficiency had come the idea of the shop. It is so very pleasing when one thing leads easily and naturally to another. If they had been two young gentlemen living together, making yoghurt and sewing smocks, the village would have talked, but for two ladies nothing could be more proper, and if they also shared a bed, only Mrs Marshall knew that, and she kept her own counsel.

So it had gone for seven years. Consciously or unconsciously, the girls had fashioned a way of life which was as intricate as the web of any spider, the nest of any wren, and of which the purpose was not much to do with self-sufficiency or sweeping a room for anyone's laws, but was a framework which would allow them to live together without hindrance and without being bored. In much the same way did the philosopher, James Mill, fashion for his son John a rational world in which to enjoy rational happiness, and only when John Stuart Mill discovered that he was not at all happy, and had a nervous breakdown to prove it, did that rational world fall to pieces. So now, in the summer of the pig's escape, did Susan discover that she *was* bored, and the intricate framework quivered.

There was a whole world outside the village, and Sue had never known it. London! Why had they never lived in London, and enjoyed the society of intelligent sophisticated people? What friends did they have? There were Jake and Edna, who owned the herd of goats which supplied the dairy. There were stall-holders at Craft Fairs, next to whom the girls might pass a day or two in desultory conversation, and never meet again until the next Fair. There were Janet's parents and Sue's family, seldom visited, their own visits dreaded.

In seven years the girls had never taken a holiday. The framework for living had become a prison. Each new activity had been undertaken on the principle of 'If this, then why not that?', and so they had encaged themselves. Bees! What madness to keep bees! And chickens – the most unlovely birds in God's creation! Agnosticism comes creeping in at once when one thinks of Him creating chickens.

Take, for instance, the process of making the hard round cheeses. The heating of the goats' milk, in its water-bath with the bobbing thermometer, to 68°C exactly, and cooling it to 32°C, the adding of the starter and leaving it, the rennet and leaving it, the cutting of the curd into squares with a palette knife (taking great care not to break it up) and leaving it. The stirring of it gently by hand while bringing its temperature gradually to 38°C, and leaving it. The ladling off of what whey one could, then draining the curds in a bundle of cheesecloth tied with a Stilton knot, opening the bundle, cutting the curd and turning it inwards, re-tying the bundle, and leaving it. And again. And leaving it. And again. And the milling and the salting and the moulding and the pressing, and the turning, and the increasing of the pressure, and leaving it, and the cooling, and the bandaging, and the storing it hanging up in bags, and the daily turning of it, and the leaving it, and the ripening, and the regular inspections against cheese-fly and cheese-mite, and the leaving it, and the blanching and application of the vine-leaves, and the leaving it, and the leaving it, and the leaving it. The time! the effort! The girls themselves rarely ate the cheeses, preferring the soft curd which was easier to make and lower in cholesterol, and they were too expensive and too unfamilar for the villagers to buy them; these goats' milk cheeses, wrapped in vine-leaves, were a loss-leader for passing trade, talking points for dinner parties which the girls would never attend; they were the possibility of an article, or at least a mention in an article, in some Sunday colour supplement.

No, they were not; they were not. They were symbols of the wasted effort by which she and Janet bound themselves together. Sue bought at the Spar a wedge of processed cheddar wrapped in polythene, and put it on the table for lunch. Janet's lips tightened, but she made no comment.

She must be fair. She loved Janet. She owed so much to Janet. She had needed someone to awaken her emotionally and to provide the security in which the awakening could flower. She had found fulfilment and protection with Janet, and she as much as Janet had created this refuge which now so constricted her. The dairy had been her own idea, a whole room converted to

21

it; she had consulted catalogues, and filled the space with gloss paint and aluminium; she had insisted on a traditional cast-iron separator with a ball-bearing in the handle to tell one how fast it was going. But needs change. Living creatures have to be allowed to grow. Even an agapanthus requires re-potting.

Their life together had become habitual. Sue only now began to notice it, and the noticing chafed her, since Janet did not seem to notice it, or perhaps rejoiced in it: perhaps it was what Janet had always intended, in which case . . . Better not to follow that thought further.

The girls took it in turns to prepare breakfast, usually a piece of fruit and a pot of tea brought up to the bedroom. Sue sat on the edge of the bed, picking a satsuma into segments, watched warily by Jan. She gazed into space, puffed out her cheeks, sighed, said nothing.

'What's up?'

'Nothing.'

'You're sighing.'

'I can breathe, can't I?'

She left the bed, propped her elbows on the window-sill, and stared out over fields. There were bullocks in the lower field, sheep in the upper. Chaffinches picked for seeds in the drive, and rooks circled aimlessly over the woods. A very ordinary morning. If a fox were to cross the field, it would give her something to say. She wished to talk, and not to. She wished everything to be as it had always been, yet she wished for change, and did not know what sort of change. Looking from this same window during the February snow, that was when she had seen a fox crossing the field, red on white (she had said to Jan) like a Japanese print, walking with one paw held in the air. It must have been caught in a trap. How *could* people? It would have bitten its way out.

It would have bitten its way out. Sue became silent; she became snappish. She began to suffer from erotic daydreams. There was a grey fog inside her head for much of the time, which, if it had a name, could be called 'resentment'. It seemed impossible to speak of her

22

discontent, because that would be ingratitude. What would she be without Janet? What would she have become? She might have become anything at all, and had not; it was all Jan's fault.

She began to perform certain tasks obsessively, watering the vegetable patch and the fruit trees every evening, keeping her head turned away so that Jan should not see that she was crying. Other tasks would be skimped; the over-watered French beans, which she neglected to pick, grew long as cutlasses. Sometimes she demanded the physical reassurance of hugs and sometimes shrugged them angrily away, still insisting that there was nothing wrong, until her behaviour alarmed them both so much that an appointment was made with the doctor, who prescribed valium. But Jan had seen enough of that during her days with the Probation Service, and tore up the prescription.

June ended bumpily. July was even bumpier. They had nobody to consult. Susan had been too young to have old friends when first they met, and Janet's had fallen away, excluded by the new intimacy. They had never discussed their relationship with anyone locally, and now could not even discuss it with each other, since Susan flew so easily into a rage or sulks, and Janet discovered that what she had always believed to be the capacity to take an objective view somehow turned easily into self-justification and blame. Although still so much in each other's company, the girls began to retreat more and more inside their own heads, but whereas interior Sue crouched amidst fog, hugging her own knees, unable to articulate even the simplest thought, interior Jan strode perpetually, restlessly, relentlessly, up and down, round and about the bare room of her mind engaged in rational argument with a thousand Susans, some remembered, some she had herself created, none willing even to respond, far less to agree, to conclude, to reach a reconciliation, to meet anyone halfway. Jan was on a hiding to nothing, heartless if she ignored Susan's evident distress, interfering if she attempted to help.

23

In August the girls won their usual First at the Flower Show for a 'Platter of Mixed Exotic Vegetables', a Second for their tomatoes, and a Second for dandelion wine. It was usual for them to win a First for elderflower in the Country Wines Section, but change was in the air that year; Susan had insisted on dandelion, and certainly elderflower was so popular with passing trade that it seemed a pity to waste a bottle on the judges at the Flower Show. In August also, twenty-three days in, the monthly account arrived from the credit card company, and was found to contain an unexpected amount of money paid to Blue Sky Travel. It was clearly a mistake, which Janet would point out when she paid the bill.

Sue turned red, and announced in a decisive mumble that there was no mistake, that she had been meaning to mention it, that she had decided that she had to get away on her own for a while to find out who she really was, and that she had booked a package tour to Crete, leaving on Tuesday. She would pay for it with her own money.

4

THE INLAND WATERWAYS
RALLY

Susan was required to check in by ten a.m. and, since the
journey would take at least four hours, the girls were up
betimes. They drove mainly in silence, Susan paler than
usual and Janet a little more highly coloured, and stopped
only once for petrol and for Susan to visit the Ladies. In
the car park at Gatwick they embraced, sitting awkwardly
side by side in the front seats of the van, and Susan said
she would rather make her own way from there, but she
looked so forlorn, standing in the car park with a heavy
suitcase, that Janet said, 'Wait!', locked the van, and the
two of them carried the suitcase together over to the
terminal building, from which came a sound as of prisoners rioting.

It was worse inside, like a beehive but without the
order. There was clearly very little room to move, yet at
least a third of the people were in a state of restless
frantic movement. Those passengers who had been lucky
enough to find trolleys pushed them about, bumping the
legs of others, burdened with luggage, who clung together in groups, terrified of being separated. 'This way!'
'Over here!' 'Can you tell me –'; there were long queues
at all the check-in counters, and desperate passengers,
already late, pushing through the lines as they tried to
discover which check-in counter they should be queueing
at, since this information was available only when one

25

had achieved the head of the line. Only a few children wept; most were large-eyed and wary, and some had been given iced lollies to keep them quiet, and these dripped on the baggage of other passengers. An Italian couple, who had queued for twenty-five minutes at the wrong counter, refused to move to any other, and after much argument won their point. Goans despaired. An elderly American in a jacket of purple and yellow checks over dacron trousers, glared in the general direction from which airport announcements were being broadcast and shouted, 'Slow down, you bitch!' Sue said, 'Don't leave me,' and the girls' fingers met and clasped over the handle of her suitcase.

They found the right counter. They stood side by side in line, fingers still clasped over Sue's suitcase, which finally had to be given up and was carried away on a moving belt. There was no time for a cup of coffee. Sue's flight was already being called, and the passengers still in the queue made little moaning motions of despair. They walked together to passport control, where Jan was allowed to go no further. Sue's hand clutched Jan's, then released it. She walked on, like Lady Jane Grey on her way to execution, turning to look back once and wave. Jan remained where she was, gazing after her. They had not been separated for seven years.

She felt no pain during the journey back. She was numb, she supposed, and there was classical music on the radio, and the route itself until Windsor was so confusing that it required all her concentration. They had closed the shop for the day, but it was three in the afternoon by the time she arrived at the cottage, and there was so much to do; it left no time for pining. She made herself a cup of tea, and read the day's post. There were orders for honey and potted rabbit, and one for a pair of men's clogs, size 9½, in dark blue with a buckle. She collected eggs, watered courgettes, and picked plums which would have to go for jam; the wasps had been at them. She carried sugar syrup in a plastic bucket down to the bees, and wondered whether she should tell them that Sue had gone away. But it was not death; it was only a fortnight's holiday; she decided not to mention it.

She made herself a poached egg on toast with a green salad, and watched television while embroidering a canal-belt, and so the evening passed. Lettuce is non-addictive and said to be calming, and the canal-belt would fetch fifteen pounds. A fortnight was no time, when one put it into perspective. The belt was of linen, folded over twice, and then stitched together. On it Janet was embroidering a band of roses. Leather buckles would be attached when the embroidery had been finished. She had the address of Susan's hotel, but not the telephone number. They had agreed that it would be of little use, since there was no subscriber-trunk-dialling to Crete, and it was unlikely that she would be able to make herself understood by a Greek telephone-operator. In any case it would be more difficult for Susan to find out who she was if Janet kept phoning all the time.

Canal people liked to dress up; they always had. Once the narrow-boats had carried the produce of factory and farm along a whole network of canals, which Janet visualised as rather like a diagram of the human circulation-system. The boats had been painted with roses and castles, and their owners had worn, when the climate and the nature of their cargo allowed, brightly decorated clobber to go with them. The belts were traditional, the embroidered patterns traditional; the girls had copied them from a museum. Now the owners of such narrow-boats as were not let out to holiday-makers were accountants, vanity publishers, solicitors with practices mainly in conveyancing, sales directors, personnel managers, area managers and the managers of suburban betting shops, local government officers, permanent civil servants who had taken early retirement, the owners of garages and of fish-and-chip parlours and of small fleets of vans selling soft ice-cream. The narrow-boats of these owners never carried coal; finery could be worn freely, and it was.

The annual Inland Waterways Rally was to be held during the coming week in Yorkshire, not far from Sykehouse, where the villages have names like Great Heck and Little Heck, and the cooling towers rise from flat fields of wheat. There would be barge races, barn dances, ox-roasts, competitions for the best-dressed boats and the best-dressed owners, and a Craft Fair. The girls had booked a stall in the marquee; they would be able to sell as many of the canal-belts as they could make and perhaps a smock or two as well. Correction: 'they' would not be there; only Janet would be there, selling from the stall which both had booked the canal-belts and perhaps smocks which both had made. On the television, a comedy programme about two octogenarians running a guest-house in Torremolinos to which she had been paying little attention, ended, and was replaced by one in which a man in a bow-tie bullied four politicians in front of an audience. Janet switched off the set, poured herself a large whisky, and went to bed.

She awoke in a panic at two in the morning, and lay staring at the blackness, trying to locate the source of her fear. Something had happened to Sue. There had been a cry of pain or terror, a call for help heard only in sleep by her, Janet, who was hundreds of miles away, utterly unable to protect, to avert – what? Her dream had not told her. She did not even know if the aircraft had arrived safely. She should have watched the news instead of that comedy programme; if an aircraft full of British holiday-makers had fallen into the Aegean, it would have been reported. What time was it? What time would it be in Crete? There was to have been a journey by coach, she remembered, from the airport at Heraklion to the hotel on the north-west coast of the island, a considerable journey at night through rocky passes, from which boulders might crash onto the road. Greek drivers were notorious. She saw as from an immense distance the two coaches, both crowded with package tourists, approach the blind corner through the velvet night, saw them meet head on like vast armoured insects, their carapaces crumbling on impact, saw the flames, heard the cries of the trapped passengers, Sue among them, smelled the burning flesh. Even if Sue were to survive the mechanical perils of the journey, she was in herself so helpless. She had not been abroad since a school ski-ing holiday at seventeen; even her passport had required renewal; she was totally inexperienced and vulnerable, unable to speak any foreign language beyond schoolgirl French. Travel documents may be lost; they may be stolen; there is always a market abroad for a British passport. Her face would go red, her hair wispy; she would try not to cry, and fail. Janet saw her, tearful and awkward, passport lost, money and travellers' cheques lost, suitcase misrouted to Istanbul, being turned away from the package hotel to shiver through the streets of an alien town, saw her beaten by thugs, pushed *in extremis* under some jacaranda or tamarisk to be discovered, days later, already decomposing, by tourists of another package. She saw herself, Jan, make the identification in a Greek mortuary before indifferent attendants. She saw, and would not see. She closed her eyes, and called up common sense, old friend, to help her. If anything had happened, she would have heard by now – but the parents are told, not the lover, when an aircraft crashes or coaches collide. Common sense turned against her, taking the side of fear, and she lay awake until dawn.

Two in the morning at the cottage was four in the morning on the sixth floor of the hotel outside Chania, where Susan lay awake in the single bed of a single room just two and a half times wider than the bed. Light shone through a glass panel set above the door, and the surface of the corridor outside was of some composition substance on which every footfall echoed. The corridor was long. Susan had lost count of the number of feet which had fallen on its surface, had ceased to speculate on the nature and deeds of those who had already called 'Good night' to each other down its full length, or gone giggling doubly into single rooms. Faintly from above her she could hear, as she had heard for many hours, the sound of disco-dancing on the roof. A notice in the lift had promised that the disco would close at four-thirty. For the umpteenth time, she pulled the sheet as high as it would go, placed the pillow over her head, and attempted to compose herself for sleep.

At five Janet managed to get to sleep, and was awakened by the alarm at seven. There was plenty to do, no time for brooding, and anyway her night fears became insubstantial in daylight. If anything had gone wrong, she would have been told, since the package had been booked from the cottage; the girls' telephone number had been written on many forms. In any case the whole point of a package tour was that nothing did go wrong; one might not enjoy it very much, but nothing went wrong, because all the package firms were members of some kind of Association; even the onset of meningitis would be dealt with, or in some way averted. She bathed, ate a bowl of muesli with yoghurt, drank coffee, and performed the morning's tasks briskly. She was at the shop by ten. In January, whether the shop were open or no was a matter of no great importance, but September is still a holiday month, and the road through the village had been designated a Leisure Drive.

It was quiet, of course: it was always quiet. Some passing trade in a Ford Cortina enquired what 'free range' actually meant, as applied to eggs, and Janet explained, not for the first time, that it meant what it said. The hens were free to range within an enclosure of wire-netting of a mesh fine enough to exclude the foxes, rats, weasels and any other predators who might wish to make a meal of them. Being hens, and bloody-minded, they chose for most of the time not to exercise this freedom, emerging from the semi-darkness of the hen-house only twice a day for expensive corn or pellets. 'Pellets for pullets, eh?' the passing trade said, and went away, well pleased at his own word-play, having bought a dozen eggs and a pot of rhubarb chutney.

At eleven o'clock a young woman of extraordinary beauty came into the shop.

She had arrived outside the shop alone in a TR7 with the hood down. She was carrying a shoulder-bag. She

30

wore sandals of soft leather over bare feet and trousers of tan corduroy which seemed to have been moulded on her. What distinguishes a description from a catalogue? *'The barge she sat in, like a burnished throne . . .'* Enobarbus doesn't even get to Cleopatra herself until line seven, and then it is only, *'For her own person, it beggared all description.'* The young woman had grey eyes under eyebrows darker than her hair, which was the colour of stripped pine. Freckles like motes of dust dancing in sunlight were set in honey-coloured skin. She wore a loose shirt of faded powder-blue linen, open at the throat, with the top button unfastened and no bra beneath so that one could see quite clearly that the honey-colour of the skin extended to her breasts, and there seemed no good reason why she should not be honey-coloured all over. She was straight – straight nose, straight back, straight gaze of the grey eyes, straight but not stiff, direct but not aggressive. She glowed. It was as if someone had made an essence of youth, and put it in a package, and this was the package.

She bought a loaf and curd cheese, pâté, elderflower wine, lettuce and cherry tomatoes. 'It's lunch, lunch!' she said. 'They told me this was a Gift Shop.'

'We don't know what else to call it. Did you see a gift? Or anything? Maybe in the window?' Janet caught herself hoping that the young woman would fancy a smock and wish to try it on, and blushed furiously.

'I thought I might look about.'

'Please.'

'Don't go away. I never mind being watched. Stay and talk to me.'

Janet had no intention of going away, and was not sure that her legs would support her if she tried. She sat on the stool behind the counter, and turned her head so as not to be caught staring when the young woman bent to look at lace.

They talked, Janet cannot now remember what about – probably about the shop and the village: she remembers that she asked, 'Do you live locally?' because of the effort she had to make to keep the question light, though it

31

seemed to her of the utmost importance. Another stool was set for the young woman, and mugs of instant coffee were prepared and consumed during a period of frozen time. The young woman did not buy a gift, though she admired everything in the shop.

Then the light changed. Clouds scudded over the sun, and the first drops of a September shower struck the street window of the shop. 'Oh God! The car! The hood's down.' The young woman jumped up from her stool, but there was already a sulky someone sitting in the car, who had arrived unnoticed while they talked, and who now left it with ill grace, and began to fumble with the hood. 'He'll break something. He's helpless. How much do I owe you?' While Janet fumbled for change (not a lot of it) from a ten-pound note, the young woman packed food and elderflower wine into her shoulder-bag.

'I'll give you a bag for the lettuce.'

'No time. I told you; he gets furious and pulls at things. I wouldn't mind, but it's my car.' And she was gone, crying, 'Don't *tug*, Giles!' as she ran through the doorway.

Aided and directed by the young woman, Giles finished raising the hood. They took very little time to do it; the powder-blue shirt was hardly spotted with rain. Janet watched. He was of medium height, swarthy, with greasy black hair going bald at the back. She recognised him as an actor from the Royal Shakespeare Company.

The two of them got into the car, and the young woman drove it away. Janet, standing just inside the door, wondered whether there might be a momentary look back, but there was not. Janet waved anyway, then returned to the counter, her legs now only too solid and heavy, while the September rain darkened the dust of the street. For Christ's sake! She was thirty-seven, and should be well past this sort of thing.

She was jumpy for the rest of the day, but again there was plenty to do, and again it was not until two in the morning that the night fears returned. This time they had changed their nature. She no longer saw Susan in peril and in terror. Quite the contrary. She closed her eyes, and

32

witnessed in the most sickening clarity Susan enjoying herself.

Susan had gone away to discover who she was. She had to have, she had said, time by herself in order to think things through. Insofar as Janet had allowed herself to visualise this process at all, it had been a vision of Susan alone, sitting on a beach-towel spread over sand or pebbles, thinking. There would be the sea somewhere, certainly the sound of the sea, and perhaps small children playing. This vision now became displaced by others most unwelcome. Susan dancing, Susan laughing, Susan frolicking in waves with others, windsurfing with others, held closely by others as she was tumbled by breakers, Susan drunk, Susan with her breasts flopping in and out of a loosely buttoned powder-blue linen shirt, Susan naked in sand, caressed, licked, squeezed, gathered up in handfuls, taken from in front and behind, sweating amid rumpled sheets, raked by nails, gasping out excited sounds of pleasure and lust, Susan, only Susan – for only she could be clearly seen behind Janet's closed lids, her partners being various and ill-defined, some female, some male, one of whom had a hairy back and a bald spot on the crown of his head.

A mile away, the church clock struck three. And four. And five. Janet lay alone in a double bed, and sweated with jealousy. Susan had gone away to discover who she was. Oh God, what if she should discover she was not Janet's?

These thoughts were not so easily dissipated by daylight. They required to be pushed away, and would return not long afterwards, disturbing the concentration required for embroidering canal-belts, for the finicking routine of the dairy, for the making of lists of what stock to take to the Craft Fair at the Inland Waterways Rally. Janet had never felt jealousy before. How could she, when she and Susan were always together? It was like having her mind taken over. Rational logical common-sensical Janet became whimpering, hysterical, vengeful. She

33

devised horrible punishments for Susan. Luckily all this took place inside her head where others could not see it.

That night she swallowed four tablets of Sleep Compleat from the Health Food Shop when she went to bed, but they had very little effect. She begun to wish she had not torn up the doctor's prescription for valium.

It was like an illness; it *was* an illness. She was sick. 'Jan, you're sick.' A sick mind, *mens insana in corpore solo*. Susan had gone away to find out who she was. It was wicked and wrong of Janet to think of Susan as being in any way 'hers'. Nobody belongs to anybody else. Nobody can be defined only in terms of somebody else – 'his wife', 'her husband', 'my lover'. People, even couples who live together, even couples who live as closely together as Sue and Jan, must respect each other's separateness, other-wise when one of them dies or . . . leaves or . . . when one of them is for whatever reason no longer there, then the other is likely to go into a decline or loopy, as loopy as poor silly sick Janet Hallas. A grip, a grip; take a grip. People need holidays from each other. Paradoxically it brings them closer. They need to . . . experiment, experi-ence, to . . . refresh, to be refreshed, to . . . Janet bit her tongue. Her mouth filled with blood. She had to close the shop early; one could not serve passing trade while looking like the Bride of Dracula. Mrs Marshall, up for the day to clean, saw trouble and went away grieving. It was the first Wednesday for several years on which she had not in some way immobilised the vacuum-cleaner. Her heart was not in cleaning that day.

Jealousy! Which of us has not at some time felt it, and been damaged and diminished by it?

She made lists, packed boxes, began to prepare in earnest for the journey to Sykehouse. It would take her mind away for a while from this madness. The Rally was to be a two-day affair; she would have to stay overnight, and Mrs Marshall would feed the hens. Jan could well afford an hotel, but that would have cut into profit. She intended to sleep in the Transit van, which would prevent pilferage of the stock, as well as saving money. Sleeping-bag, therefore; it was in the attic with the camp-bed. Once she and Sue had shared it during a walking tour in the Lake District. A thick pullover or cardigan, and boots lined with lambs' wool; September nights could be chilly. The knitted cap which Sue had bought her against the snow in February. She found it in the handkerchief drawer with a lavender bag, and stood for half an hour, in a maze, just holding it. Spare underwear, because one never knew. Most of the actual stock would have to be packed as late as possible, since smocks crease easily and the butter on potted meats may run. Dare she take comb honey, which could, if overheated, be even runnier? – it was so very popular; she ought to try. No vegetables, eggs or bread of course, but as wide a selection as possible of the jams, chutneys, pâtés, cheeses, fudge, anything not quickly perishable, because they caught the eye, and one would take orders as well as selling what one had brought. Catalogues! There were only a hundred copies left of the cyclostyled sheet which the girls used as a catalogue and there was no time to get more run off. One day they would have a printed leaflet with decorative designs in the margin. Toothbrush and toothpaste, nail-brush and soap, mouthwash in case of bad breath (she had a horror of bad breath), soluble aspirin, perhaps Arpège in an atomiser to give her confidence. Towel. Instant coffee. Mug. Torch. If she took apples and cheese for herself, she would not need an evening meal. Had Sue been coming with her, and particularly if they had a successful first day, they would look for a place for dinner in *The Good Food Guide*, but such places do not always welcome women on their own, and anyway it would be a waste.

For the last two evenings before her departure, Jan did not watch television while she embroidered, but instead played a tape of the love duet from Act Two of *L'Incoronazione di Poppea* over and over, sometimes weeping quietly. Meanwhile Susan, in the newly-built package-tour hotel near Chania, was attempting to persuade the Tour Leader, whose resemblance to the lady who used to

35

make lampshades out of human skin at Dachau grew every day more pronounced, to allow her to go home early, but was refused.

The roof of the marquee had stripes of grey which had once been white, and brown, which had once been purple. It had seen many wedding receptions. Both roof and walls had been thriftily patched, but they were good sailcloth; they still kept out the wind and rain. The marquee had slipped downmarket, but it had further to slide. There would be years of fêtes and flower shows and country auctions before it was cut up to cover junk in yards or refurbish deck-chairs in a municipal park.

It had been erected in a meadow beside the canal, and was surrounded by stalls, which looked like a shanty town around a cathedral. These outside stalls, being open to weather and unprotected by stewards from drunks and teenagers, cost less to rent; they were poorly stocked, and most were not craft stalls at all, but sold remaindered knitwear, cheap sweets, and all the rubbish to be found at any Saturday market. The real craft stalls were inside, but the stallholders paid a ten-pound premium.

Entrance to the marquee was by ticket, for the organisers of Craft Fairs, resembling Messrs Sotheby and Christie in this if in no other way, take money from those who buy as well as those who sell. From ten that morning, first in a straggle then in a gaggle, the punters had been admitted, and now milled about. Inside there were stalls lining three of the walls and formed into hollow rectangles in the centre, so that the punters could circulate freely. On the fourth side was a table set with oilcloth, but this was not devoted to the display and sale of crafts. Teas, sandwiches wrapped in clingfilm and hot pies were sold there. The catering at the Fair was a concession. Despite the nature of the occasion, there would be no nonsense about nutritious foods. Customers who required raw carrots and wholemeal bread brought their own.

These were the traditional British crafts to be found at the stalls within the marquee.

There was a man cutting Non-Toxic Alphabet Letters from linoleum individually at customers' requests, and a man with a portable furnace operated on bottled gas who fashioned glass into the shapes of animals, birds and butterflies, all of which seemed to have been designed by Walt Disney, and a man in a sombrero two feet wide, running a raffle for the Self-improvement Society. There was a black lady in a red bandana selling ethnic African objects made in South Korea, and a Chinese lady selling ginseng and plastic chopsticks. There were Make-Your-own-Sheepskin-Rug Kits, which consisted of small pieces of sheepskin and the equipment for sewing them together; one had to assume that they were either the trimmings of rugs which had been sold at other Fairs, or else that the skins of sheep had been deliberately cut into bits in order to be stitched together again. There were standing mirrors set in padded leather, and ceramic walking-sticks, and leather hair-slides for ladies, and cushions which seemed to have been covered in poodle-fur. There were personalised glass beakers and hand-framed knitwear and hand-crafted hidework. There was hand-decorated coin-jewellery and homemade orange-and-pineapple marzipan and variegated ivy sold in terraniums which looked like shrunken conservatories, as if some form of bonsai treatment had been applied to the glass and its anodised metal framework. There were Victorian lace cushions and *cache-mains* (all washable), and christening robes (fully lined, with bonnets), and stoneware mugs and candlesticks with a notice reading 'Please Handle the Pots'. There was stall upon stall of clocks and silver charms and rings and chains and enamels and unpolished semi-precious stones. There were mice pincushions and mohair sweaters and home-baked cakes and marmalade, and there were salad bowls and pen-sets of turned wood. There was a stall selling *découpage*, which proved to be biscuit-boxes with pictures of Prince Philip and the Queen Mother (not necessarily together) cut from illustrated magazines and stuck on the lids. There were paper flowers and silk flowers and pressed flowers in leatherette frames, real shell bangles and maps of the county of Humberside framed in wood. There were soft toys and wooden toys and ethnic toys and kites. There were buckets painted with traditional boatmen's designs, and a stall reserved for the Philatelic Society of Goole, but this was untenanted. There was weaving yarn, and useful objects made from it, such as table-runners and wall-hangings, and there were shuttles for weaving the yarn, and bobbins attached to skipping-ropes in case the weavers grew bored or needed to exercise their legs. There were unpaid volunteers from Save Britain's Heritage selling cassettes of birdsong and the conversations of whales. There were rag dolls and wooden hobby-horses and night-dress cases and make-up bags and shower-caps (all hand-stitched) and herb-pillows and pillows embroidered with the words 'Paul All Love' and perfumed flower plaques. There was Janet with a selection of clogs and smocks, canal-belts and speciality foods, and next to her a young man selling early musical instruments.

Rebecs and recorders, crumhorns and cornamusen, Glastonbury pipes, an Appalachian dulcimer and a plucked psaltery were set out on the table in front of him, and a huge wooden serpent was propped up behind him. 'We never sell anything but recorders,' he had told Janet, 'but the serpent attracts people to the stall,' and Janet had replied, 'It's the same with smocks, to tell you the truth.'

In fact very few punters so far *had* been attracted to the stall, and he had sold nothing, not even a recorder. This had aroused feelings of guilt in Janet, since she herself had been doing well with comb honey and potted hare. She had taken to giving him small apologetic smiles when making a sale, and had felt his eyes on her while she was taking an order; it had been like eating chocolate biscuits with a spaniel in the room. Usually stallholders next to the girls at Fairs sold more than they did, and feelings went quite the other way.

38

'I'm sorry.' she said, 'It's a bit quiet this morning. I
expect it'll get better.'

'That's all right. If you've got a high unit cost, you don't
have to sell many.' It was true that none of the Early
Musical Instruments was priced at under twenty pounds,
but the young man did not sound confident. 'We make
them up from kits, you see, so there's two hundred per
cent profit if you don't include the labour.'

' "We"? '

'My partner and me. Usually we do the Fairs together,
but he had to go to Rotterdam. It's the first time I've been
on my own.'

'My partner's in Crete.'

'Festival of Baroque Music. It was an emergency. One
of the girls we know in a Consort got thrush. Bob's very
versatile. Shawms – any woodwind. Lutes. Anything but
keyboard. Self-taught. He's always ready to oblige if
anyone drops out. It's a bloody nuisance, as a matter of
fact. It's not easy, looking after a stall when you're on
your own.'

'I know.'

'You miss the company. I mean, if there's somebody
with you, then you don't feel so self-conscious. And I've
been wanting to go to the loo for half an hour. I expect
you've noticed me looking at you.'

'I thought it was envy. Do you want me to keep an eye
on the stall for a bit?'

'Would you?' He was already on his way. 'I shan't be
long. If anyone shows an interest, just keep them talking.'

Luckily nobody did show much of an interest. Many of
the punters seemed to be embarrassed by early musical
instruments, and looked away; the stall was beyond their
expectations, and they could not deal with it. The young
man explained on his return that such behaviour was
usual. Sophisticated punters, if they arrived at all, would
do so in the late afternoon. 'You just have to stick it out,'
he said. 'I mean, if things get really quiet, Bob usually
plays something – a bit of Bach . . . Couperin . . . Handel
. . . the Beatles even. "Yesterday" always goes down

39

well. He's got a medley for cornamuse if we're desperate – "Yesterday", "Penny Lane", "Michelle" – it never fails.'

'To sell?'

'To get them round the stall. We take up a silver collection, and there's a few that linger.'

'You don't play yourself?'

He shook his head. 'I did woodwork at school and technical drawing; they didn't encourage the musical option. I do like listening, but I've never mastered an instrument. When we make up from the kits, Bob does all the tuning. I do shaping and gouging out.'

Janet said, 'I used to play the recorder once, but it was a long time ago.'

His name was Alan. He was twenty-three years old. After leaving school, he had spent two years with the Midland Bank, and then a year helping Bob and Rachel in their Wholegrains Shop while he was still trying to find himself. When Bob and Rachel had split, Bob had gone into early music, which was his real interest anyway, and taken Alan with him. Alan was not an employee because he was not paid wages. He and Bob were partners; they shared the work and shared the profits, and since he lived at home he could always survive even when there were no profits, which was sometimes the case owing to problems of cash-flow because of Rachel's having taken most of the money from the sale of the lease of the Wholegrains Shop to start a Juice Bar in Chester. To sell at all, and build up a mail-order business, they needed a showcase, but Craft Fairs were not ideal; they did better at Music Festivals, particularly those held at universities, and had lived for a month on what they had made at Lancaster.

Janet felt a sharp twinge when he spoke of the year spent finding himself because it reminded her of Susan in Crete, but the situation seemed so different, and anyway he had ended up in Crafts which must be a good sign; not even in her darkest moments could she imagine Susan taking the reverse path and ending at the Midland Bank. And he bloomed so in her company, losing his awkwardness and insecurity, getting her cups of tea and taking over the stall while she herself went in search of the loo, during which time he sold three pots of plum-and-almond conserve and a box of fudge. Then, when the narrow-boat people began to arrive in earnest, and there was a run on canal-belts with orders for clogs and a couple of rich boatwomen wanting smocks held up against their bodies and even, encouraged by their husbands, to try them on there in the marquee, then Alan left his own wares and came to work at her side, crying up the cheeses and the potted meats as if he had tasted them, clapping the soles of the clogs together as he explained to passers-by that wood allowed the feet to breathe, outlasting leather and outperforming it on beach or Nature Trail.

'You're wonderful.'

'I love selling things.'

'Look, I'll have a go with a recorder if you like.' She played *Jesu, Joy of Man's Desiring* very carefully though not very musically, drawing it up out of the memory of her schooldays as from a well, and achieved a small crowd, one of whom, a teacher from Hebden Bridge, took the instrument from her, performed immeasurably better, and bought it. Janet was possessed by triumph. She had forgotten Susan entirely.

At the end of the day she had taken two hundred and fifty pounds, more than she and Susan had ever taken on the first day of a Fair. Alan had sold only the recorder and a dozen ocarinas at three pounds each, which he produced from a carrier bag in the last hour, explaining that he despised ocarinas and there was no profit in them, but a few were always brought in a bag in case things got slow. He did not seem upset by his lack of success, but clearly shared Janet's pleasure in hers, and refused a commision. It was taken for granted that they would spend the evening together.

They put away what remained of their wares, locked their respective vans, and wandered forth. Most of the tenants of the cheaper stalls outside the marquee had also packed up and gone, leaving only those selling baked

41

potatoes, ice-creams, hot dogs and hamburgers. It was a quiet evening, which the boat-people would give over to pub-crawling and visiting from boat to boat; the Ox-Roast and Old Tyme Dancing would be tomorrow. The Rally was being held where the New Junction Canal crosses the River Went on an aqueduct before making a T-junction with the Knottingley Goole Canal. From that junction, for two miles in all three directions, the narrow-boats were moored stem to stern on both banks of each canal like a huge colony of water-insects.

'Water-boatmen!'

'Sorry?'

'They're a kind of insect. They scud about over the surface of the water, and suck the blood of fish. Only these have all pulled over to the side, and look as if they're eating into the bank.'

People were always saying things Alan didn't understand. 'They're not real canal people,' he said. 'They're just week-enders.'

There was a September chill in the air. Janet had decided finally to bring both a pullover and a cardigan, and was glad of it. She wore the first and carried the second, and it seemed appropriate that Alan should also be wearing a polo-necked pullover of an identical navy blue. They walked together through the dusk along the tow-path. The narrow-boat people were bustling about their traditional tasks, switching on portable transistor radios, opening packets of crisps and twiglets, drinking gin-and-tonic on deck, and shouting to each other across the water. Some children were making a bonfire out of bits of broken fencing and cardboard boxes which had contained light ale. The smell of pines and woodsmoke mingled with that of fried onions from the hamburger stalls by the marquee, and, cutting for a moment through the sound of Neil Diamond singing 'He Ain't Heavy; He's My Brother', Janet could hear an owl.

Alan said, 'We look like brother and sister,' and Janet took his hand, and they walked for a while, side by side, swinging their joined hands, and then thoughts of Susan

42

did come back in a rush since it was what she and Susan might have done if they could have been sure that no one was watching.

They found a pub, *The Jolly Waterman*, with tables outside and a performance by the Narrow-Boat Players just about to begin. The Players were a company of six who travelled the canals in summer in their own narrow-boat, performing in parks and the gardens of pubs some simple story, with songs and ensemble dancing, of Canal Folk and their unremitting struggle against capitalist exploitation. The Company had recently lost its Arts Council grant; this had increased its militancy without diminishing its energy. The struggle this year was that of the Jolly Cleggswood Boys against the exploiting mine-owners; last year the Boys had been from Rochdale and their exploiters clothiers, but capitalist exploiters as a class are much of a muchness, and the same songs did for both, with the wording only slightly altered. It was all highly enjoyable. Janet and Alan drank white wine by the glass and ate long sausages with strong mustard, tapped their feet to the ensemble dancing, hissed the mine-owners, shouted encouragement to the Jolly Cleggswood Boys (two of whom were girls owing to the exigencies of casting), and joined in the militant choruses, along with the rest of the pub's customers, the Jolly Inland Water-ways Rally Boys, not one of whom was earning less than twenty thousand a year.

It became accepted between them, without any word said, that Alan would not be sleeping in his own van. Janet was glad; it would protect her from wakefulness and frightening thoughts. There was just one moment of doubt when the door of the Transit was unlocked, and Alan said, 'I suppose I ought to clean my teeth,' but Janet said, 'I don't think I'll bother,' and the moment passed. They kept the door open while they unrolled and spread out the sleeping-bag, pushing back the boxes and racks of what was still unsold to make room for the two of them. Then they shut and locked themselves in. There was a light in the roof of the Transit, but neither switched

43

it on. They would have to undress sitting down. 'Have you got enough room?' 'Yes. Have you?' Janet could hear Alan pulling the polo-neck over his head; if arms were to be waved about, perhaps only one of them should do so at a time. Her eyes began to adjust to moonlight through the glass in the upper half of the door. She heard Alan getting his shoes off, then he lurched suddenly towards her and kissed her in one eye, having misjudged his aim. She held him, and was comforted by the skinniness of his chest. *Like a skinned rabbit* – but a rabbit, of course, would not be so white. How did they manage that, to get the fur off so cleanly, and leave the inner membrane covering the flesh? He fumbled at his jeans, and she let go of him to complete her own undressing. Perhaps a cloud had passed, because the moonlight seemed stronger now, and glinted on that white skin on which the rabbit-skinner had left, perhaps out of pudeur, a tuft of dark fur to blur the genitals. Alan kissed her again, and this time he did not miss her mouth. She held him with one arm, pulling at her tights with the other, then drew him down slowly; it seemed natural for her to take the lead, and not at all strange, though this was certainly her first time with a man. Alan lost his balance as he was pulled downwards, and landed with a thump, half on top of her and half beside. 'Bob says I'm easily swayed,' he said, and giggled.

It was a new experience. It was not unpleasant. When she thought of it, it was not all that new. The penis was new, but really it was only another piece of throbbing anatomy, to be felt and stroked. One could not feel it to be a threat, since Alan was not a threat. He was kissing her neck, and stroking the side of her face, and moaning. None of this was new. She moved her hand about his chest, discovered a nipple, squeezed it and felt it stiffen. Alan said, 'Christ! Christ!' She moved the hand on downwards, caught one of his, and moved the two hands together down the length of her own flank to the thigh, then inwards. His fingers fluttered, caught between gentleness and urgency. She could feel his sweat against her body, and his nose pressed into the side of her face,

44

his tongue moving against her cheek, searching for her mouth. Then everything, which should have gone into the most languorous slow motion, began to happen much too quickly. It was clear that Alan had at least a theoretical awareness of the necessity of foreplay, but even the most preliminary exploration seemed to excite him much more than it did Janet, so that hardly had his fingers achieved her labia than, uttering little cries of consternation, he heaved himself fully on top of her, and came at once.

'Alan?'

'Sorry. I always come too quickly if I'm really attracted to someone.'

Janet was not sure that this was an adequate excuse, but it seemed to be enough for Alan, for he rolled off her and almost immediately fell asleep. If this is heterosexuality, Janet thought, it certainly isn't what it's cracked up to be. But she did not blame him, and was not truly disappointed. Somehow she would have to ease him into the sleeping-bag, and then herself beside him, or they would both freeze. It was strange that she had not bothered to clean her teeth, when she had a horror of bad breath.

During the night, as was bound to happen when they were lying so close, Alan became drowsily tumescent, but she licked his nose, and told him to turn over because he was snoring, and, only half awake, he dutifully turned and slept on. 'Like brother and sister' – *for he himself has said it, and it's greatly to his credit.* So many memories of school! First the recorder, and then *Pinafore.* Moonlight turned to dawn, and Janet lay awake listening to the parking lot come to life around the van, and thought of Susan, but her thoughts were warm and loving thoughts with no jealousy; it had all been sick, that, just sick.

In the morning, neither was embarrassed. The feeling of companionship remained. They sold less, but Janet had less to sell. As the stall-holders close to them began to pack up, Alan said, 'Shall we stay for the Ox-Roast?' but it wouldn't do. There was the shop to open, and Sue would be back at the end of the week.

*

45

There were no more bad nights of the few remaining. Janet arrived at Gatwick early, and waited for ninety minutes before Susan came through from the Customs' Hall, very stiff and self-conscious like a child being met by its mother after the first day at school, looking about with only small movements of the head as if she were unsure that Janet would be there, and was determined not to show disappointment if she were not. Then she saw Janet at the barrier, and as the girls' eyes met, Jan knew that whoever Sue had found out she was, that person was, after all, still Jan's.

They walked in silence to the van, carrying the suitcase together as they had done before. As Jan unlocked the van door she said, 'How was it?' and Sue replied, 'Don't ask,' and then, as they were leaving the car-park, 'It was awful.'

Sue maintained the silence for much of the first stage of the journey home, but she held Jan's hand, only releasing it to allow her to change gear. On the outskirts of Windsor she said, 'How was it with you?'

'Not good,' Jan said. 'Not good at all. I missed you.'

'Well, I've brought you a present. I expect you'll hate it.'

What Janet did not yet know, and only later came to find out, was that spermatozoa are persistent little fellows, carrying as they do the determination of the race to survive, and that even those deposited prematurely at the mouth of the vagina will attempt the long struggle upwards, and that the most persistent may succeed.

5

BREAKING THE NEWS

She missed one period, and then another. Susan would have to be told.

She decided to make a trial run by telling Mrs Marshall. 'I think I may be pregnant.'

Mrs Marshall had been standing on a kitchen chair in order to reach cobwebs with a feather duster. She climbed down slowly, giving Janet's statement time for consideration. 'When did that happen, then?'

'September. At the Craft Fair.'

'Careless!'

'You don't go to a Craft Fair expecting to sleep with someone.'

Further consideration. Mrs Marshall was known for fair-mindedness. 'Right. You don't. Bloody bugger, that is.'

'It was only the one time. I never thought. . . .'

'You don't. It's the one-timers get caught more often than not in my opinion. Ripe for it, you see. And you're thirty-seven.' She shook her head. 'A bugger, that is, in every respect. Have you told her?'

'Not yet.'

'She'll have to be told.'

'I thought you'd advise me.'

Mrs Marshall took the duster to the kitchen window. 'Bloody ladybirds all over the place!' The ladybirds retired at this season to the cracks of windows to hibernate. 'I hate a mess.'

'I don't mind the ladybirds.'

'You want to get rid of it? I went to term with mine.'
Mrs Marshall had borne two boys out of wedlock. Both
were a credit to her, one in the police force, the other at
agricultural college. 'Doctor's surgery's the place for that.
I've no secret potions.'

'I don't know.'

'Lady doctor. Has to be confidential. She's well used to
such matters. Give you better advice than I can.'

'Abortion's not as easy as you think. There have to
be medical reasons.' Mrs Marshall grunted. 'Anyway, I
wouldn't go to Dr Barnes for an abortion. There's an
Advisory Centre at Oxford. I used to send enough of my
own clients there when I was a Probation Officer. I'm
really not sure what to do. I could be mistaken. It would
make sense to have a pregnancy test, I suppose. It's all
so embarrassing.'

Mrs Marshall said, 'You could do with a child. Save
you treating each other like children. Brought my two up
on my own. Embarrassment, that's no consideration.'

Sue said, 'But you're thirty-seven. Isn't it dangerous?'

It had not occurred to Janet that having a baby at her
age might be dangerous. She said, 'I do think I want to
have it, though. The feeling's been coming on me.'

'Of course we're going to have it. As long as it's not
dangerous. We'd better look it up.'

' "We"? Love, it's me that's pregnant.'

'Don't be pedantic, Jan. Of course you'll do the actual
having; there's no help for that, though I do envy you, I
must say. Still, I'll be there, holding your hand; they can
hardly keep me out. Do you think we could have it at
home? Women used to.'

'I'm not sure it's allowed.'

'And you'll have to breast-feed it, I suppose, until it's
weaned; we don't want any of that bottle nonsense. But
we'll both bring it up. It'll be our baby.'

'I thought you'd be jealous.'

48

'I might be later.'

'How much later?'

'I might be now if I thought about it. So I've decided not to think about it.' Like Mrs Marshall, Sue was given to honesty. 'But I expect I shall.'

'Oh, love, love!' Janet hugged her. 'It wasn't much to write home about. He was a nice boy, though. Nice nature. He said we were like brother and sister.'

'Must have had a very incestuous home-life.'

'He's an only child.' It seemed important to describe Alan as he was, so that Susan should not blow him up out of all proportion, but Janet discovered that she could no longer remember what he looked like. 'Sort of skinny. I thought of you.'

'While . . .?'

'No, not while. I didn't think of anything much while; it was over so quickly. I'd been thinking of you before, and I thought of you again after, in quite a different way. Before . . . well, I was the jealous one actually. Horribly. Ugly. All that first week, lying awake at night, thinking . . . wondering. . .' Janet had not spoken of her jealousy before; she had been too ashamed of it.

'Was that why you had it off with this boy? Because you were jealous of me?'

'No.' Janet considered further. 'Not directly, anyway. Not getting back at you. I liked him. We were both lonely. He'd been very helpful. He was awfully young. It was such a relief to be enjoying myself after all the . . . I was grateful to him.'

'All the what?'

'Night thoughts. Bloody agonising. Fevered. I kept imagining you with . . . you know. . .'

'With whom?'

'Everybody.'

'Doing what?'

'Everything.'

Susan giggled. 'You are silly. Tell me what I was doing, and we'll do it together.'

'I'll light the fire.'

49

Jan put a match to the firelighters, and the two girls sat side by side on the chesterfield in the dark room, watching the fire take hold and then blaze up. Sue put her hand on Jan's stomach, and held it there.

'It's hardly six weeks. You won't be able to feel anything yet.'

Sue let her head slide sideways to rest on Jan's shoulder. 'I don't know how we're going to tell your parents,' she said.

The doctor said, 'How old are you?'

'Thirty-seven.'

'Yes, I see. What a muddle! Well, I've signed the forms before, though I don't like doing it, but I suppose your age is a consideration.'

'What forms?'

'Green forms. For an abortion.'

'But I don't want an abortion.'

'You want to have the child adopted?'

'I want to have the child, and keep it.'

'Ah!' The doctor put down her pen. She had recently returned from the British Medical Association's Conference in Jamaica, and her nose was peeling. 'It's not my business, of course, except inasmuch as anything to do with your pre-natal state of mind *is* my business. . .' Wilfully Janet's imagination produced a picture of the inside of her mind as a nursery, hygienically clean and with a lot of pink fluffy towels. 'Anything which might create anxiety. Or, for that matter, dispel it. Let me put it this way; does the father know?'

'No. Why should he? I only met him once.'

'Ah!' again. The tips of fingers placed carefully together. The peeled patch on the doctor's nose seemed to have a freckle on it, which was now illuminated by October sunlight. 'Forgive me. One does hear. . . . I'm sure I've read about it somewhere. Women who advertise for men to impregnate them. Women in their late thirties,

50

professional women, beginning to fear they may miss the experience of motherhood. I wouldn't expect it in the village.'

'*Sunday Times*. Last month, I think. There was a play about it at some theatre. It's nothing like that.'

'But you only met the father once? There's no possibility you may be mistaken?'

'Do you mean "mistaken", or do you mean "hysterical"?' A small voice inside Janet said, *"Don't offend her."* She would need the doctor on her side. 'I'm sorry; I don't mean to be snappish. I don't think I'm mistaken. It's true he never penetrated, but I've missed two periods, and I started feeling rather sick at tea-time yesterday. Odd, that! I thought it was supposed to be in the morning.'

'Oh, no; it can be at any time. Nausea.' A note made. 'All day sometimes. It's not at all pleasant. Luckily it only lasts nine weeks.'

'Christ!'

'There are tablets if it gets unusually bad. Never penetrated, you say?'

'He got over-excited.'

'Well, it has been known. You didn't wash immediately afterwards, I take it?'

'We were in the back of a Transit van.'

'Ah! Will you be seeing him again?'

'I might bump into him at a Craft Fair. He sells early musical instruments.' It began to seem to Janet that there were some circumstances which only became more unlikely the more one tried to explain them. 'It was an accident. I wasn't expecting it. For obvious reasons, I'm not on the pill, but he wouldn't have known that.'

'Oh, quite!'

'I didn't intend it, but now it's happened, I don't want an abortion, not unless something's wrong. It's nothing to do with the father. There's no reason for him to be told. I intend to have the baby, and Miss Burt and I will look after it. I'll be an unmarried mother, but there'll be two of us.' She decided to spell it out. It was important

51

that there should be no misunderstanding. 'Practically speaking, the child will have two parents. Both women. It will be a stable family situation.'

'Ah!' Third time. The doctor was clearly being careful to avoid value judgments. Janet supposed that they were taught that at Medical School.

'I'd expect Miss Burt to be present at the birth. We'd both expect it.'

'I think it may be a little early yet to discuss all that.' Suddenly the doctor smiled, and it was like being brought out of the street into a warm room. 'Though really, my dear, I don't see why not.' The pen moved briskly over paper. 'I want you to see the obstetrician as soon as possible. As you say, we want to be sure nothing's wrong, and you are thirty-seven, so he'll arrange an amniocentesis.'

'What's that?'

'They take a sample of the amniotic fluid, and test the protein. Shows up any abnormalities – spina bifida, Down's syndrome, that sort of thing.' Janet stared at her. She read the Sunday papers and the *Guardian*, watched television; she knew about such matters, knew herself to be more at risk than a younger woman would have been, but found herself alarmed at the matter-of-fact manner of this lady doctor. 'Don't worry about it. Every mother does, of course, but don't. Abnormals are very rare. You've no family history of that sort of thing, have you?'

'I don't think so.'

'Make sure for me, will you, please?' The marks on the paper were made so quickly. Was the doctor writing words at all, or was it merely a form of confidence-giving? 'You'll come to me for all the ante-natal. They run a clinic at the hospital, but I don't like my mothers traipsing into town. Waste of time and money.'

'Do you have many mothers?'

'Four or five. They come and they go. I do one after-noon a week. It's better than your coming to surgery in the usual way and mixing with the other patients. Never know what you might catch. Now. . . . 'Notes completed, peeling nose lifted, friendly grey eyes behind tinted glasses. 'My nurse will phone about your appointment with the obstetrician. Meanwhile, no smoking please, and alcohol only in moderation. And I'd better have a urine sample, just to make sure.'

'I've brought a urine sample.' It was in a wine bottle, carefully corked. Usually the girls recycled bottles for their own wine-making, but Jan was disposed to be generous. 'You can keep the bottle.'

Janet's mother said, 'Oh, my dear, I'm so delighted,' and would have kissed her, but Janet moved away.

'So am I, mother, but are we delighted for the same reason?'

Janet had driven alone to Cheshire. She had promised Susan that she would stop for coffee at a service station, but she had not stopped for any reason. She had driven fast, ignoring curtains of dirty spray from lorries, overtaking Jaguar and Porsche, the drivers of which had become first astonished and then competitive, working herself into a rage as she drove, and had arrived early to find her parents still at lunch, so that she had been obliged to make small talk until she could speak with her mother alone, which had been even more enraging.

It ought to be possible to talk simply and directly with one's parents, and if that were not possible (as it seemed not to be), then one should be able to treat them with the friendly courtesy one extends to mere acquaintances, and not consider oneself obliged to inform them of every major change in one's personal circumstances. In fact, one arrived in a rage, and blurted out, 'Apparently I'm pregnant', over the washing-up, and one's mother had the impertinence to announce that she was delighted. How dared she be?

Janet had never told her parents in so many words that she and Susan were lovers, but she had assumed that, after so many years, they knew and had accepted it. And they did know; they *had* accepted it. All the Christmas presents, the birthday presents for darling Susan, the invitations to come and stay together, the shared room provided when they did! They had not wanted to be told any more than Janet had relished the prospect of telling them, but they had known, and no mere pregnancy of Janet's could or should allow parental expectations to go skittering back to square one.

'Why are you delighted, mother?'

'It's natural. A woman my age wants a grandchild.'

'Will dad be delighted too?'

'Of course he will.'

'That's all right, then.' Janet dried a glass carefully. 'You take it for granted I'm not having an abortion.'

'If you were, you wouldn't have come to tell us.'

'Right.'

It came to Janet's mother that she had been put without any warning into an emotional minefield, and must contrive to get them both out of it without an explosion. Years ago she had despaired of grandchildren. Now it seemed that there was the chance of at least one, but she must not show delight, far less relief, since that would be taken as disapproval of the way in which Janet had so far chosen to live. Support, then, must be her line, support in what was to be without putting down what had been. But who was the man, and what would happen to Susan? There would have to be a settlement, and it should be generous. Perhaps Susan should be given the cottage and the business, to set up with some other girl of her own age, and Janet would move nearer home, where she could be properly looked after.

'Is he someone you've been seeing regularly? The father.'

'He's somebody I met exactly once.'

'Oh!'

'Puts me in a new light, doesn't it?'

'Janet, will you please stop being hostile when I'm trying to take things in?'

'I've seen the gynaecologist. It'll be June the fifth.

54

Round about then. And there are no indicated abnormalities, though one can't be too careful at my age.'

'We ought to get Dr Grindlay to take a look at you.'

'I'm with the village doctor. Dr Barnes. She trained in midwifery. She says she's pleased with me.'

'Does the father know?'

'Of course not.'

'Shouldn't you tell him?'

'No.'

'You're not saying it was rape or anything?'

'No. He's quite a presentable young man. Much younger than I. We spent a night together while Susan was away. I found him rather a comfort.'

It all seemed very unfair to Janet's mother. If Janet was capable of spending nights with young men in this casual and unconcerned way, why had she not done so long ago, and produced a whole family of beautiful grandchildren of both sexes in a detached house in Knutsford with a swimming-pool at the bottom of the garden?

'He should be told, Jan. He has some rights.'

'He has no rights.'

'Surely there are legal – ?'

'No.'

'The child is half his.'

'No.'

Janet's mother began to shake. She found herself to be in the gravest danger of giving way to anger and disappointment when all she had wanted to do was to offer support. All about her, the hidden mines began to hiss and bubble in the kitchen floor. 'I don't know why you're behaving so unreasonably,' she said. 'All I've ever wanted for you is that you should settle down, and have a family, and be happy and fulfilled.'

'I have settled down. I have a family. I am happy – as happy as most people. I am fulfilled. I thought you'd accepted that, you and dad. Now that I'm to have a baby, I suppose I shall be even more fulfilled. Two happy people and a child – isn't that what you've wanted for me? You didn't imagine anything else would be changed? You couldn't know me, could you, and really believe that one night in a Transit van with a callow young man would make any real difference? Sexual orientation, mother, is not a matter of whom you fuck; it's whom you love.'

Mrs Hallas struck her daughter across the face, and Janet turned, left the kitchen, picked up her suitcase from the hall, walked out of the front door, got into the car, and drove back, two and a half hours of mainly motorway driving, to the home she shared with Susan.

Janet's mother went into the back garden to find Janet's father, who was raking dead leaves off the lawn.

'Jan gone? I heard the car.'

'She came to tell us she's pregnant. I didn't handle it very well, I'm afraid. She got rather cross. I hit her.'

'Ah! How does Sue feel about it?'

'We didn't get as far as that.'

'Probably should have started with that.'

Janet's mother felt a strong inclination to bring off the double by hitting Janet's father as well, but he saw the intention in her eyes, and grinned. 'Come on,' he said. 'We'll go indoors. I expect she wound you up. What though the day be lost? All is not lost. We'll write a letter.'

Janet's mother thought, not for the first time, that acceptance was a great deal easier for Janet's father, and that he might feel altogether differently if their homosexual only child had been a son.

Please remember that this encounter between Janet and her mother took place back in November, 1974. Nowadays parents, not only in the metropolis but even in Cheshire, have been educated by the quality press and by television into a much more liberal attitude towards the sexual preferences of their children. Even daughters. Haven't they?

As for the village, it said you never could tell, but the village was used to children born out of wedlock, and the girls were well liked in the village.

56

(6)

RABBITS

It was coming up Christmas. Sue bought a crib at the Oxfam Shop, and the girls decorated it together. Usually they made only a gesture to the season – a wreath on the door, holly behind the tops of pictures, Christmas cards fastened to strips of ribbon which were hung up on either side of the ingle-nook, a small pile of wrapped presents from family and friends to be opened on Christmas Day (their own presents for each other being hidden in various traditional places) – but this year, since the prospect of nativity was so much in their thoughts, they had decided to celebrate Christ's birth in more style.

On December 6th, Jan's breasts had definitely begun to swell, and the curve of her abdomen was visible to more than the eye of faith. The nausea had persisted, as Dr Barnes had foretold, but not unbearably, so that the debendox tablets prescribed against it remained, most of them, in the phial. Nevertheless the girls had decided that their special celebrations had better delight the eye than the belly; their Christmas dinner should be spartan, perhaps a broth of lentils with a little dry sherry in it to mark the occasion, and poached fish after. But then December 21st passed without sickness, and December 22nd the same, and it seemed (although this had been foretold also by the doctor) as if the Almighty had made a special dispensation, and there was a last-minute expedition to the village for turkey, and the making of a multitude of mince-

57

pies, and a telephone call to Jake and Edna, the goat-breeders, to join them on Christmas Day for a feast.

On Christmas Eve, Mrs Marshall was brought, as for the last five years, from the village by her younger son to drink champagne by the fire, and nibble at fingers of toast spread with tapenade. Sue took the crib from the window, and set it before the hearth, and the three ladies sang *Holy Night* and what they could remember of *Unto Us a Child is Born* tearfully and tipsily together. Ralph Marshall, arriving to find his mother with a tear-stained face and tousled hair, did not know what to make of it all, but she hugged the girls, saying, 'Oh, I have enjoyed myself!' and sniffed contentedly in the car all the way back to her caravan, where she heated up a tin of mulligatawny soup, and went to bed. Foxes prowled round the caravan at night, and one caught his nose in the empty soup-can, but Mrs Marshall slept peacefully though all the commotion.

It was the best of times. With the short days and cold weather, the range of the girls' activities became narrower. The shop was only opened on Fridays and Saturdays, and not even then if the girls did not feel like it, since passing trade was hardly to be expected in January. Cheese-making was cut sharply back, the demand now being only local, nor did Jake and Edna's goats give as much milk in winter, and anyway goats' milk freezes well. Sue would still often go into the dairy, and sometimes take Jan with her, but only because she enjoyed looking at it, and wished to share her enjoyment. The dairy was her favourite room, designed by her, all white and silver, the colours of Paradise; the room was so clean and pretty, she wished Jan were allowed to have the baby there.

Hens and bees had still to be fed, but these were not arduous tasks, and there were no fruits or vegetables from the garden to freeze or preserve. As for the garden itself, although the writers on gardening insist that there is always much to be done, the truth is that, when the ground is soggy, one cannot get onto it, so the much never is done, and not much harm seems to come of not doing it.

Jan herself was suffused with a feeling of well-being, and moved in haze of content. She had not yet grown heavy, not so as to be uncomfortable, but knew herself to be a mother, and looked about at her world with a mother's eye, like a dove which has chosen its nesting-place and soon will lay. Sue, when asked in the village how Janet was, said that she glowed like a ripening fruit, and this was repeated in butcher's, Spar and chapel as evidence of a poetic sensibility. Most of what work there was to be done about the house had passed to Sue, who did it joyfully. What Jan most enjoyed was to sit and watch. She sat in the conservatory by the Calor gas heater, and watched the valley and the further hills. She sat in the kitchen by the oil-heater, and watched the tits at the nut-bag. She sat in the living-room by the log fire, and watched the flames. She sat up in bed against pillows in the morning, and watched Sue bring in the breakfast. She watched snow fall, and the rain which melted the snow, and the wind moving the branches of a pollarded willow like a fan, and was content. She was not tired, she wanted Sue and Mrs Marshall to know, not at all tired, but she was languorous; she enjoyed her languor. On February 6th she felt the child within her kick for the first time, and Sue, called from shaping hamburgers, put a hand on Jan's stomach, and was sure that she too felt the baby move, and burst into tears of joy. There were many joyful tears during this time.

Later in February, Susan went alone to the Crafts Fair held over two days at the racecourse at Haydock Park. The girls had at last replaced their catalogue with an attractive, locally printed leaflet, designed by Jan, illustrated with line drawings by Sue, and had great hopes of pepping up the mail order. She looked about the hall for a stall selling early musical instruments, and found one in the diagonally opposite corner. There were two people behind it, one a fat man with a beard, the other a skinny young man who looked like a rabbit in denims. The stall was too far away for her to be able to tell whether it was doing much business, but in the evening, about forty minutes before closing-time, the bearded man picked up what seemed to be a shortened walking stick, blew into it, and played a *bourrée* by Handel which quickly drew a crowd. Sue herself drove home when she had packed the van, to spend the night with Jan. She did not mention the early music stall, and Jan did not ask.

She returned early on the morning of the second day, and was in her place by opening-time. She looked across to see whether the early music men had returned also, and caught the skinny one staring at her.

During the afternoon, he left his stall, and approached her. 'I thought your friend might be here today.'

'She's looking after the shop.'

'On Sunday?'

'Oh! . . . No, not today. She's looking after the house today.'

Susan's feelings were mixed. She wished to talk to him, and wished him to go. She was curious to know him better, and anxious not to encourage him to presume upon acquaintance. She certainly did not intend to tell him that she knew who he was.

As for the young man, he remained hanging about in front of the stall, but seemed unable to think of anything more to say. 'Would you tell her I was asking after her? Alan. We met at Sykehouse.' A man and his wife stopped to look at clogs, and the woman picked up one of the new catalogues. Susan said, 'Please keep it if you like. We take orders by post.'

The woman put down the catalogue at once, and moved on with her husband. Alan picked the catalogue up, and Susan tried to think of a reason to ask him to put it back, but could not. The girls had discussed for a long time whether to use their own address or that of the shop in the catalogue. Finally they had decided to use the home address, since the mail-order business was conducted from home, and there were many days in winter when they would not go into the shop at all, and orders would lie there unfulfilled; they would create ill will. Alan said, 'It's pretty, isn't it? You just had a bit of paper before.' He put the catalogue carefully in his pocket. 'You'll remember to give Jan my regards?' *"Jan!"* He presumed too much. She wished she could tell him so. He took a step away from the stall, and back. 'She's awfully nice. I really enjoyed meeting her,' and was gone while Susan fumed internally.

The best time gave way to a worse time which was still not a bad time. Janet grew heavier, uncomfortably so. She slept late most mornings, went to bed early at night, and often took a nap at around tea-time. Susan would watch her as she slept, sometimes reaching out to touch her hair or gently stroke her belly.

In the garden snowdrops were followed by crocus and the brightly coloured iris reticulata, and tulips made little humps in the frosty ground as a preparation to pushing through. Then there were scilla and the smaller daffodils, primrose and cowslip, a wash of anemones in the rockery, and March was nearly over. The conservatory grew warmer in the thin sunlight, and Janet would be placed in a reclining chair there, covered with rugs, while Susan was busy about the house. She took to leaving the chair, and moving slowly about the garden, mooning over bulbs and the promise of leaves on hawthorn and crab, and feeling the flower-buds of the weeping pear between her fingers. She would rest her belly against the bars of the wooden fence at the end of the garden, and watch the lambs in the neighbouring field, until pursued by Susan like a busy scolding squirrel, who would wrap her in a duffel coat and push her back indoors. It was on one of these occasions that Janet suddenly felt her womb contract and, terrified that she might be miscarrying, swayed and became dead weight, so that Susan was hard put to hold her up. 'What is it, love? What's wrong?' Susan said, bracing one heel against the wall of the dairy as she

61

struggled to keep Janet upright, and Janet remembered that Dr Barnes had foretold this also, and at about this time, and took some of her weight off Susan by gripping a branch of the willow, saying, 'Nothing to worry about. Just limbering up,' and allowed Susan to lead her back into the house.

Janet placid, Susan shrill; Janet confident and content, Susan forever anxious. Janet hungry, and Susan – well, Susan kept her company and put on weight. Susan, it has to be said, was something of a pain in the arse during this period of the pregnancy, forever buying books on natural childbirth, prescribing new exercises, diets or ingenious ways of breathing, devising lists of what Janet must be careful to avoid, which included deep underwater swimming. This last set Janet into a gale of giggles, and since uncontrolled giggling was also a prohibited activity, Susan became extremely cross, cried, threatened to leave forever a home in which her self-sacrifice was not appreciated, and had to be coaxed back into good humour by kisses and caresses, which is not easy when one's stomach is the size of a telephone-box.

Jan herself was never cross. Her expanding uterus pressed up against the underside of her lungs, and she became short of breath but never of temper. Her ankles swelled, and Dr Barnes worried about her blood pressure, put her on diuretics so that she was forever pissing, and warned Susan to watch out for fits, but there were no fits, and the condition passed. April gave way to May. Hawthorn and crab apple were in bloom, grass required cutting, and everywhere the sun drew flowers out of beds which had been bare six weeks earlier. The bees swarmed, and the swarm was lost. Susan grew thinner, running everywhere, attempting to minister all at once to shop, dairy, garden and her pregnant friend until Mrs Marshall appeared early one Monday morning, and said, 'I've had enough of you playing silly buggers. I'm coming in three times a week, and Edna can look after the shop.'

It seemed that the baby now left no room in Janet's stomach for anything but acid. She began to suffer from heartburn, and fancied only bread and milk, while urging Susan to keep her own strength up by hearty eating. Many tempting dishes were prepared, and found their way to the chickens. A suitcase was kept permanently packed, and whenever a contraction was felt there would be the consultation of watches, in case others should follow it at regular intervals. Janet had become monstrous, enormous, a bovine creature, and could only sleep propped up on pillows. Nevertheless the girls continued to share a bed since, particularly at night, each required the reassurance of the other's presence.

There are odd similarities between the last few weeks before a birth and those before a death in some case of terminal illness when the patient is protected from pain by drugs. The patient herself, everything done for and to her, drifts from day to day placidly towards an unavoidable event which will happen when it happens. It is the lover, husband, favourite child who frets and behaves badly, unable to accept that what is so important and so unavoidable cannot, when it comes, be shared, but only watched. Susan struggled to be a support to someone who, except when in actual danger of falling over, did not require support. To Janet the changes within her own body seemed natural so that she did not worry about them, but Susan's knowledge of the processes of childbirth was entirely theoretical, ill remembered from biology lessons at school, and buttressed now by all the books she had bought which were often contradictory in their conclusions. She worried constantly about Janet's body. It did not seem natural to her at all, but a very ill-devised mechanism for an event which could easily go wrong, in which case she herself, Susan, was bound to be blamed. And if that event should go right, as was to be hoped, then she herself wished to be, and to be seen to be, part of it, if only as stage-manager. Susan lay awake at night, listening to Janet's laboured breathing, and felt envy.

Janet imagined the baby inside her, fully fashioned by now, blind but curious, moving its arms and legs in liquid, touching the walls of her womb and the placenta, exploring its world insofar as its world would allow it room to do so, a water-creature attached to her by a cord inside her body, alive, able to hear her own heartbeat, to listen to herself and Susan in conversation and the natural noises of the garden and hillside, so that later, after it had been born, it would be able to recognise those noises. She played music to it on the tape-deck in the evenings, the Monteverdi 'Love Duet' of course, and piano sonatas by Haydn and Mozart, and the double violin concerto of J. S. Bach. She persuaded Susan to read aloud, a chapter a night from *The Railway Children*. She would look at pictures from Susan's books of babies curled up in cut-out sections of women's bodies, and could understand why Dr Barnes and the midwife (whom at last she had been allowed to meet) always referred to 'baby' never to 'her' or 'him': none of the babies in the pictures had any badge of sex, and hers would have no sex until its sex could be seen. She did wonder sometimes whether baby was comfortable upside down.

Janet's waters broke at six in the morning while she and Susan were still in bed, and ruined the mattress. They were at the hospital by seven-fifteen. The baby had chosen an inconvenient time. The midwife, who already knew Janet and had been introduced to Susan, would not come on duty until eight, and the sister on duty was a stranger to both.

Susan said, 'Where would you like me to wait?'

'Oh, there's no need to hang around.'

'I'm her friend.'

'Yes of course, dear. It's very kind of you, but there's really no need to wait. It often takes longer than you expect, and you can see for yourself, we haven't the facilities. Why don't you come back in a couple of hours? Or phone?'

'She wants me with her.'

'You're not a relation?'

'I'm her friend.'

Janet said, 'I'd like her with me, please.'

64

'I'd really rather not stand about in the corridor arguing when you're in labour. We can't let everybody into the Delivery Room; you must see that. We do make an exception for husbands if they really want to be there, but I'm bound to say that most of them don't.'

Susan said, 'I'm her friend. We live together. We do everything together.'

Sister's expression said, 'Hardly everything,' but Susan had met lips like that at the Teachers' Training College, and continued resolutely, 'Dr Barnes promised I could be with Janet during the delivery. She's spoken to the obstetrician. And the midwife knows.'

'Oh!' Sister consulted a clipboard, flicking over pages. 'Well, it's extremely irregular, but it seems there's no objection. Anyway I'm afraid I must ask you to wait here for a while. Miss Hallas, please come with me. We have things to do.'

Susan said, 'She doesn't want an epidural. That's in the notes too.'

This time Sister's expression clearly meant, 'We've got a right couple here.' She had never approved even of husbands in the Delivery Room. It was all fashionable nonsense. They read about it, or saw something on television, and thought they wanted it. The middle classes got their own way too much in her opinion. The last husband had fainted and had to be dragged by his heels from under their feet and left in a corner. 'A bath and an enema were what I had in mind,' she said, 'if you've no objection. Just wait here. We'll find you a gown, and someone will call you when your friend is ready.'

Susan said, 'Thank you. I bought a tin of Kooltabs to wipe her brow,' receiving Sister's third expression, which was of infinite patience, straight between the eyes before Janet was whisked away down the corridor. Since there didn't seem to be a chair or bench, she leaned against the wall, and waited as she had been told until a trainee came back for the suitcase.

*

Susan, as she tells it, cannot really describe the birth, although she was a witness to it. Her impressions were confused at the time, and have become more confused since.

She was provided with a gown and a small mask of gauze, a piece of which she managed to get at a very early stage into her mouth, and dared neither to spit it out nor swallow it. The Delivery Room was kept warm so as to be at a safe temperature when baby emerged. Susan began to sweat lightly, though more from nervousness than the heat. There was a bank of lights in the roof above the bed. She supposed that when they were switched on the room would get even warmer. Janet had been dressed in a backless gown like a corpse laid out for the bereaved to view. They had no delicacy, these hospital people; they were so unwelcoming.

At first the girls were left alone together, and Susan held Janet's hand, and made what conversation she could which was not much. She had been instructed to count the time between contractions, and to ring the bell for the midwife when they were three minutes apart. Sweat trickled into Susan's eyes when she looked at her watch, and she began to fear that her measurement of time might become inexact. Round swept the second-hand. Three minutes! Was it? Wait! Nothing hasty; keep looking at the watch. 'Aaaah!' from Janet. Three minutes! A drop of sweat ran down Susan's nose, and splashed onto the face of the watch, obscuring the second-hand. Oh God, what if the baby should arrive before the midwife? 'Aaah!' Three minutes! The bell! It was obviously broken; it made no sound at all. Again! It would ring, of course, somewhere else, in some no doubt completely deserted office, but shouldn't it give some indication at this end when it was pressed that it did actually work? 'Aaaah!' Again, again! Bloody bell, bloody stinking useless bell! The midwife arrives with the trainee in tow, and observes calmly that there is no occasion to panic. They measure the expansion of Janet's cervix. The trainee seems to be as nervous as Susan. Have they, then, brought some totally unqualified

66

and inexperienced youngster to assist? Wipe Jan's brow with a Kooltab, Susan, and keep your mouth shut. Janet lies with her knees up, her gown lifted, only her top half covered, all else exposed. How humiliating it all is!

Calm down, Susan. You are privileged to be here. This is one of the most important experiences of your life and Janet's life. Just remember it's all beautiful, as the books say, and don't swallow the gauze.

The overhead lights have been switched on, and the room becomes much hotter. Susan's light sweat is now profuse, though not as profuse as Janet's. However, Janet will not be required to go home when it is all over, still wearing sopping undies and with great wet patches under her arms. Susan, Susan, banish these ungenerous thoughts. You are here to be supportive. Beam loving thoughts at your friend. Sue grabbed Jan's hand, and held it tightly. Sweat ran down both arms, mingled, and collected in a pool on the waterproof undersheet.

Because the epidural had been refused, there was clearly pain, more than there needed to be. Susan took the responsibility for this pain upon herself, since it was her book on natural childbirth which had advised refusing the epidural. She took the responsibility, but she could not feel the pain. Janet felt the pain. She screamed. It was horrible. Yet the screaming seemed in some way actually to assist the process of pushing out the baby; certainly the midwife took it for granted. Scream and push! Breathe! Scream and push! Breathe! Were they screams of pain at all? Susan was reminded of medieval soldiers in Japanese movies, who screamed to frighten the enemy. Screams of rage. At whom, at what, at women's lot? She looked at Janet's face, swollen, distorted, sweating, the hair all dishevelled. Scream and push! Breathe! She looked at Janet, and saw a Japanese in a leather helmet shaking a spear.

'Good girl, good girl! There, it's baby's head. Do you want to see the baby's head, dear?' To which of them was the midwife speaking? Obviously Janet was in no position to see into her own womb. Susan looked. The top of the baby's head appeared, like a dark mushroom poking its way out of compost. The midwife took a pair of scissors, and, as casually as if she were snipping into the rind of a rasher of bacon before grilling it for breakfast, cut the perineum, fastening each side of the cut with little clips. Susan stared at her, appalled. 'Have to do that, dear. Don't want a rip, do we? Couldn't control it,' and then to Janet, 'Heave, dear! One big heave!' and with a scream and heave from Janet the baby's head emerged. 'Now we're on the home stretch,' said the midwife, and Janet looked through her own legs and saw her baby's head.

Susan's first thought was that the rabbity young man must have negro blood in him; the baby's head was so dark. But then there was another big heave to get the shoulders out, and then the rest of the baby slithered out easily, and could be seen to be white, or more exactly a shiny pink and in fact rather rabbity itself, though probably all newborn babies looked like that. Nothing that the midwife now chose to do, nothing that the trainee would do under orders, could any longer appal Susan. It had all turned out well, and Janet was well, and had done well, and the baby was well, quite clearly well; it announced its own advent with a noise more pleasing to the ear than a choir of angels. They put a tube up its nose, no doubt for some excellent reason, and snipped the umbilical cord with those same wonderful scissors, and sealed it at both sides with more of the wonderful little clips, and wrapped him, and gave him to Janet to hold, and Janet was smiling, and holding him against her breast, and his wonderful head turned, and his lips, his lips were searching and finding, and Susan ached, she ached through tears to hold him herself, but knew that this was Janet's moment, and was glad, and reached out a hand, and gripped Janet's sweaty hand, and the midwife took the baby away to a table on the other side of the room, no doubt again for excellent reasons, and there was a last contraction, and the afterbirth slipped out onto the plastic undersheet, and even though it looked like a piece of liver which only a butcher on the verge of bankruptcy would try to sell, it too was wonderful, because Susan knew from the books that it had been the baby's lungs and mouth and shock-absorber, and anyway it had been part of Janet who was of all beings the most wonderful.

And now Janet was not smiling at the baby, but at Susan, directly at her, and Susan began to feel as if they had shared something after all. 'Well, I'm never going through that again,' Jan said. 'If we have any more, you'll have to do it.'

7

NOTHING OUT OF THE ORDINARY

The Inland Waterways Rally, which changed its venue annually, was held at Ellesmere Port that September, but the girls' attitude to Craft Fairs had altered now that there was Butch to consider. They had lost their enthusiasm for these two-day occasions. Instead they had taken stalls at Stratford and Chipping Camden and the smaller local Fairs, and had sold enough to cover their costs as well as stimulating interest among the tourists in their mail-order business. The girls had despatched clogs to Wichita Falls and a smock to Nagasaki. Susan had dreams of going international. The Inland Waterways Rally was very small beer in comparison.

At three months old, Butch no longer resembled a rabbit. He had been christened 'Jonathan Victor', 'Victor' after Janet's father and Jonathan because both Janet and Susan liked the name in itself and also thought it went particularly well with 'Hallas'. Jonathan Hallas – he could be an actor, writer, painter ('the Jonathan Hallas Retrospective'), musician ('An Evening with Jonathan Hallas'), even a country solicitor. After considerable reasoned discussion they had decided simply to register the name, leaving baptism for a time when Butch was old enough to be capable of making up his own mind, but Mrs Marshall, upon whose sense of what was fitting in village matters they had long relied, had insisted on a christening and furthermore, although she was staunchly chapel herself, that it should be in the village church which was more suitable to the girls' social status. 'Being as you can't be married, you'd better have him christened. You have to do some things right in this world,' she had said. The girls, both of whom had been conventionally christened themselves, had been secretly relieved by this decision. They had both bought hats to wear to the church, and Mrs Marshall had worn a hat which had not been seen in the village for twenty years and reeked of lavender. She had been godmother, with Jake as godfather, and both the Hallas and Burt parents in uneasy attendance. Susan's parents did not know what to make of it at all. They had not known what to make of Susan ever since she had begun to live with Jan, which was particularly galling because up to that time they had always known exactly what to make of Susan, and had usually made it.

Alan arrived in early October. Bob brought him. There was an Early Music Festival at the Warwick Arts Centre, and they took the opportunity to drop in.

Luckily Susan was alone in the house. Janet had decided to spend the afternoon in the shop, taking Butch with her in the carry-cot, since he was bound to demand feeding at some time. This had left Susan free to have a go at the plums – chutney, a conserve with almonds which always sold well, bottling, the stewing and freezing of plums for their own use through the winter. They had intended to experiment this year with candied plums for the Christmas trade, but Butch's advent had put an end to such notions; they were too tired. Butch himself had been introduced to plums that very day, just a couple of teaspoonsful of purée at lunch as a supplement to the breast, and had seemed to relish them. He relished everything, was a model baby, seldom cried except for a reason, smiled often, both took and relinquished the breast as gently as a unicorn, could now hold his head up, and was always ready to be entertained by whatever the girls might offer in the way of entertainment from a musical mobile to bobbins on a string. He allowed himself to be

71

bathed and changed without fuss, and best of all he did not play favourites, appeared to enjoy being cuddled, held or carried about in a sling, but did not mind which of the girls held him. It was all joy. Even the business of changing him was a joy. The girls, being able to afford it, bought disposable nappies. It was an economy really; there was always too much to do in the kitchen without having it cluttered up by bits of terry-towelling, either boiling or drying. Disposable nappies were no problem, provided that one did not try to flush them down the loo, where they would get stuck in the S-bend or clog the septic tank.

Susan was particularly glad of the absence of nappies (and presence of plums) when Alan and Bob arrived. Without them there was nothing on the ground floor to indicate that a baby lived in the house.

Alan said, 'We looked for you at Ellesmere Port.'

'We didn't go.'

'I got your address from the catalogue. It seemed silly to be so close and not call in.'

Susan wiped hands sticky with plum juice on her apron while calculations went clicking over in her mind. She turned off all three hobs. Luckily nothing was at a critical stage. They would have to be given tea, after having come so far, and perhaps a quick trip round the garden.

'I'm afraid Janet's in Evesham. She won't be back until late, and she may even stay over.'

If they needed the loo there was the downstairs loo by the conservatory, used for cleaning up after gardening and with nothing pertaining to Butch left about in it. She must get rid of them by five at the latest; it seemed unlikely that she would be able to make an opportunity to telephone the shop and tell Janet to stay away until called. The Warwick Arts Centre is not, of course, in Warwick, but on the outskirts of Coventry. Therefore their way to it would not take them through the village; they would not pass the shop, glancing through the window to catch a glimpse of Janet giving suck. If Alan were to see Butch, he might start counting backwards and then the fat would really be in the fire.

She gave them a brisk tea with home-made bread and honey, showed them the garden, and pushed them out at ten to five, pleading the pressure of plums. On their way back to the Warwick Arts Centre, Bob said to Alan, 'They're not very friendly, your friends,' and Alan replied, 'It's her friend that's friendly.' There was silence for a while, thoughtful on both sides, and then Alan said, 'I wonder why they had that plastic mobile screwed to the back of a chair.'

Janet was troubled when Susan told her of the visit. 'He is quite nice really,' she said. 'You'd like him if you gave yourself the chance.'

'It's not a question of niceness.'

'I don't see why he shouldn't know.'

So they had another of their reasoned discussions, which lasted all through Butch's evening feed, and his bath time and through putting him down. He caught some of the anxiety which underlay the reasonableness, and was fretful, which was not at all usual for Butch.

'You see?' Susan said. '*He* knows.'

Alan sent a card at Christmas, but did not receive one from the girls in return, even though he sent it early and printed his address on the inside. He had taken trouble with that card, since it would be making a statement about him, and had hesitated for a long time over an expensive reproduction of *Virgin With Marmosets* by Brueghel the Elder until persuaded by Bob that the card Miró had designed for UNICEF would not only be much cheaper but would better represent him as the kind of person the girls might choose as a friend, someone who combined concern for the underprivileged with a civilised enjoyment of modern (but not too modern) painting.

Then in March he came himself without warning on a day when the wind sent columns of rain sliding down

73

the hillside and the sound of raindrops on the window was like hundreds of old gentlemen rustling the pages of the *Financial Times*. He was wet to the skin, muddy jeans clinging to his calves, his soggy duffel coat weighing him down, even the change of underwear in his canvas over-night bag wet through.

This time only Janet and Butch were at home, and Susan was in the shop. They did not see his arrival, and were surprised by his knock at the door. He stood there in the doorway. Behind him tulips were bent almost to the ground and the necks of daffodils were broken. He looked ill, as well as cold and wet. He said he was just passing and had thought he would come and see them. This was clearly untrue. Nobody was ever just passing the girls' house, which was half a mile along a bumpy track off a minor road, across two cattle-grids and down a hill through woods. Janet sent him upstairs to take off his wet clothes and towel himself dry. She sorted out a pair of jeans, a woollen shirt and a sweater of Susan's which she thought might fit him and a pair of socks and slippers of her own. She wrung what water she could from his own clothes, and hung them in the kitchen to dry. She made him tea and, since he was hungry, bacon sandwiches. Alan sat on the floor and played with Butch. He gave no indication of wanting to count backwards.

A corner of the living-room had been converted into a play-area, with a rampart of padded boxes and crates enclosing a blanket and waterproof sheet over the stripped pine floorboards. Butch was crawling now, and on the way to walking – which was to say that, although he could not actually walk, he could stand if supported and move one foot in front of the other in a kind of mime of walking which (the girls said) was like Marcel Marceau. For Alan he was performing a trick newly invented in which one arm was waved in front of him until it struck a rubber ball, whereupon he would crawl after the ball and strike it again until brought up short by one of the ramparts. Alan's part in the game was to turn him round to face the opposite rampart when this happened, and reposition the ball.

'He's very bright, isn't he? Has he got any teeth?'

'Of course he has teeth. He's – ' Janet stopped herself from saying how old Butch was. 'He's got six. Six front teeth, two at the top and four at the bottom.'

'What does he eat?'

'Oh, he's tucking into a varied diet these days. Boiled egg, buttered toast, stewed apple, cauliflower au gratin, chicken, cut off the joint with two veg. All mashed, of course. He's working up to stuffed olives, but he hasn't got there yet. And he's very keen on gravy, both to eat and to wear.'

'Does he cry a lot?'

'Hardly at all.'

'They mostly do when they're teething. So I've heard.'

'Butch doesn't.'

'All right, he's perfect. I accept that.' He moved round to the other side of the ramparts, where Butch had again achieved *impasse*, and this time set him on a diagonal course. 'There you go! Do you think I could stop over for a night? It seems pointless to take all this trouble drying my clothes if they're going to get wet again immediately.'

Surely he didn't imagine that he could take up again where they had left off, not in her own home with Susan in the house, to say nothing of the baby? 'I thought you were on your way somewhere,' she said.

'Only to London. It doesn't matter when I get there. I just took off. I didn't say when I'd be back. It's a slack time, you see. We only make up the kits to replace what's been sold, and the stock level's quite high at the moment.'

'You're not expecting to sleep with me?'

'I wouldn't mind, if you wouldn't.'

'Alan, it happened once. That doesn't mean it has to happen again. I think we should be clear about this. You and I, we were among strangers, I was upset for various reasons, feeling rather insecure, and I liked you; we'd become friends. We still are, I hope. It happened, and I

75

don't regret it, but this is my home.' She decided to spell it out. 'I live with Susan. We're lovers.'

'Yes, I thought you might be.' He looked at her and then at Butch. She had gone too far; he would make the connection. Butch, having reached the opposite corner, had managed to turn himself about. He saw Alan looking at him, and began the crawl back. Alan held out one hand, and wiggled the fingers, and Butch, when he was within reach, took a grip of them.

Outside daylight had turned to dusk. Susan arrived and parked the car, but the wind was louder than the noise of the engine; what with the wind and the double glazing, neither Janet nor Alan heard the car's arrival nor the sound of the latch of the gate as it was opened and closed. Susan had not expected her arrival to be heard in this weather, and came quietly to the window of the living-room so that she might enjoy looking in to watch, unobserved. She looked through the window, and saw by the light of the fire Janet and someone in her own clothes playing with Butch.

Susan entered the living-room in a state of shock. Jan saw at once what she was feeling, and said, 'Alan, will you go upstairs please, and wait in the bathroom? Don't come down until I call for you.' Alan left the room immediately without question; agreeability was one of his virtues. Butch, deprived of fingers, let out a howl, and had to be picked up. Jan said, 'He arrived just over an hour ago. He was soaked to the skin; I had to find something for him to wear. He says he's on his way to London, but that's obviously just an excuse; he must have come specially.'

'Why?'

'I don't think he has many friends. He's asked if he can stay the night. I haven't said 'Yes' or No', but I don't see why not. He can't be expected to hitchhike to London in the dark in this weather. He can have the spare room.'

'And Butch?'

'He didn't seem to know about Butch; that's not why he came. But he's bound to make the connection.'

76

'And when he does?'

'What harm can he do? I think we should tell him?'

Meanwhile upstairs in the bathroom, sitting on the loo, Alan made the connection.

Three different people with three different pre-occupations.

Janet was right about Alan. He didn't have many friends. Take away Bob, and he didn't have any. He had wanted a life with some meaning to it; that was why he had left the Midland Bank. He wanted to be with people who did creative and satisfying and worthwhile work, and to do such work himself. Making and selling early musical instruments was creative in a way, and satisfying when he was actually doing it, but for much of the time, owing to the uncertain nature of the market, he was not actually doing it. Bob could make music itself as well as the instruments, and was often asked to do so, while Alan lived with his parents and waited for occupation. The people he had known at school, the people of his own neighbourhood, did not share his interests or his desire for a meaningful life, and Bob's friends were not interested in him because he was not a performer; no relationship of Alan's with any of Bob's friends had come to anything, because they quickly grew bored. He daydreamed. When he had met Jan at the Inland Water-ways Rally, she had been at ease with him and he with her, and during the two days she had not seemed to grow bored. He had helped her; they had walked by the canal, and made love romantically in a Transit van. Janet was a daydream come true, and he wished to prolong her. She had a friend already, so they would not be going to bed again, but he could accept that. Going to bed was secondary. What was important was that they should all be friends; Alan would fit in. As for Butch, he had not begun fully to comprehend the fact of Butch; his daydreams had never gone so far. He would re-examine

77

the situation and cherish it when he was alone in bed that night.

Janet herself was as secure in her motherhood as she had been in the later stages of her pregnancy. There is nothing like breast-feeding for promoting an overall state of well-being, and although Butch was on to solids now, he was still not above a bit of suckling whenever he felt the need for comfort or reassurance. Janet was sure of herself, sure of Susan, sure of her child. This equilibrium could have been destroyed by illness or poverty, but she was not poor and none of them had been ill. She had enjoyed her encounter with Alan, was relaxed in his company since he himself so clearly enjoyed hers, felt some gratitude to him as having been at least the starting point for Butch, and did not see him as a threat.

Susan saw Alan as a threat. Are you censorious? Do you believe that Susan's reaction was selfish and self-protective, that she feared that he might take her place as Butch's father? Think what you will; that was not it. Susan did not consider herself to be *in loco patris* or wish to be; she was content to be Butch's other mother. Her protectiveness was for the three of them, the family unit of Susan, Janet and Butch, the two mothers and their son, and it was instinctive. Susan's instinct told her that society would destroy this admirable arrangement if it could. She had no precedents to justify her fear, for this, remember, was the autumn of 1975, when no learned judge had yet removed a child from its lesbian mother as being an unfit person to rear it on account of her blatant sexial deviancy; those cases were yet to come. Nevertheless she was afraid. The unit survived by being private and self-contained. Alan was at the least an intrusion into privacy, at worst a person with the right to be included within the unit and to refashion it.

In the morning Alan did not speak of his night-thoughts, but asked if he might help to feed Butch with scrambled egg, and made a fair job of it, getting at least half into Butch's mouth. 'Must be a change for him being fed by a man,' Alan said, 'but he doesn't seem to mind, does he?' and Janet quickly explained that Butch never minded being fed by anyone; the food was more important to him than the feeder. It was clear to Janet that Alan had done his sums, but she hoped it was not clear to Sue.

What was clear to Susan was that she was being made to feel like an outsider. In any ordinary two-parent one-baby family in which the father goes out to work, however much he may be determined to help and does help, there is a division of roles. Most obviously the father remains a two-handed being while the mother becomes for much of the time one-handed, telephoning, making lists, preparing food, washing dishes and drying what cannot be left to drain, pulling up bedclothes, moving toys from where they may be stepped on or tripped over, unpacking carrier bags, all with one hand, the other being taken up with holding the baby in any of many possible positions. This had never happened in the Hallas-Burt household; one of the girls was always free to hold Butch while the other performed some necessary task, and Butch never minded who. Now Alan was asking Janet for permission to feed Butch, addressing observations about Butch's behaviour to Janet, behaving as if Butch were Janet's baby instead of Jan-and-Sue's baby. Mrs Marshall never did that, nor Jake and Edna, nor anyone from the village, not that anyone from the village ever came to the house except in the case of an electrical emergency or some such. Only Janet's parents did that, and they, of course, would welcome Alan if they got to know of his arrival on the scene.

They must not know. No one must know of him. He must be packed off to London and never allowed to return. Susan was ready to move house if necessary, and would tell Jan so.

Meanwhile he was packed off to a bath while the girls washed up the dirty dishes. Susan said, 'When's he going?'

'Some time, I suppose. He'll want to get to London in daylight, and I shouldn't think he has anywhere to stay.' Susan grunted. Alan, it seemed, was one of those who depended on the kindness of strangers, an irresponsible person, the merest sponger. Janet said, 'It's stopped raining. Why don't you show him the garden?'

'He saw it in October.'

'He could help you feed the hens.'

Feeding Butch was bad enough. Was Janet determined to encourage Alan to feed every bloody thing? Feeding things was a way of making oneself part of a household; it made one feel as if the things belonged to oneself, and soon the things felt that also. 'Show him the dairy,' Janet said. 'Do something welcoming.'

'I don't feel welcoming. I want him to go.'

'I could see that. I hope he can't. It's not like you to be so cold. He can't do any harm, love. He'll be off on his travels again some time today, and that will be it.'

'No, he won't; he'll call in on his way back with a present for Butch. If he hasn't guessed already, he soon will. We'll never get rid of him.'

'He lives in the north somewhere. He works there, making clavichords from kits; you've met his partner. All right, he needs friends; he's lonely. That doesn't mean to say he's going to move in with us.'

'We've never had a friend before that one of us has liked and the other hasn't.'

'You could like him if you gave yourself the chance.'

Susan was afraid she might break a plate, so she took Butch into the living-room to cuddle him. Since it was not his time for being cuddled, and anyway Susan was in a state of extreme tension, he grew quickly restive which made matters worse. But when Alan came downstairs wearing his own clothes from which most of the mud had been brushed, and announced that he would have to leave before lunch, she brightened and asked if he would like to look around.

The wind had dropped, the rain held off, and watery sunshine was reflected from the puddles on the patio.

From the village about a mile down the valley came the sound of church bells; it was the one Sunday in four when matins was celebrated in the village church. Susan and Alan fed the hens and looked for eggs, then Alan changed into slippers and was taken to see the dairy. He was shown the cast-iron separator with its singing ball-bearing in the handle, the cheese vat with its outer and inner jackets, the butter press and moulds, the cheese-press, the curd-cutting knives, the acidmeter; the uses of rennet were explained to him, he was given information about critical temperatures which went in one ear and out the other, and he was warned against yeasts. To Alan, attempting an enthusiasm he did not feel, the room seemed as unwelcoming as its designer, all steel and white paint and scrubbed surfaces. He said, 'It's like an operating theatre, isn't it?'

'It's meant to be like Paradise.'

'You don't make blue cheese, then?'

'Why do you say that?'

'Corruption. Letting Satan in. Wouldn't do in Paradise.'

This was a genuine flight of fancy, which might have won him respect from some of Bob's friends. It was Alan's bad luck that it should have come to him while in the company of someone whose cast of mind was more literal than literary, for all Susan replied was, 'We don't make blue cheese actually, because goats' milk isn't suited to it,' and left a silence to be filled.

Alan looked about for distraction, and was glad to see a piece of equipment he could recognise, a bat with a handle all fashioned from a single piece of hard wood. 'Butter pat?'

'It's a Scotch hand.'

'It looks like a butter pat. What's it for?'

'It is a butter pat. It's called a Scotch hand.'

Alan said, 'Having a son. It gives meaning to your life, doesn't it?' At these words, Susan knew that Jan was quite wrong, that Alan would never give up, that he would always be arriving uninvited and might even try to move in with them, so she hit him on the back of the

81

head with the Scotch hand, and he fell down on the floor. Her action was immediate, following immediately on her interpretation of what he had said, which was also immediate. Something, as Mrs Marshall would have remarked, 'came over her', so that she did not give herself time to consider that her interpretation might have been mistaken, and that Alan's question might have been the beginning of a conversation intended to reassure her that he would never intrude upon her relationship with Janet, but would be grateful if he were allowed to visit Butch from time to time and be informed of his progress through life. Alan was a gentle and agreeable person, anxious for good opinions and disturbed by strife; the second interpretation is at least as likely as the first.

We do not know what Alan meant, and never shall, no more than Susan, who stood above his body trying to take in what she had done and saying, 'I'm sorry. I didn't mean to hurt you. Please get up.' It was true that she had not meant to hurt him, any more than one means to hurt a fly by swatting it. When swatting flies, the question of hurting them is not a consideration. One only wishes to rid oneself of the flies.

Since Alan did not get up even when requested to do so, Susan knelt beside him in order to persuade him further. He was lying oddly, face flat on the floor, in a manner which was not at all self-protective. It occurred to her that the floor of the dairy was of quarry tiles over concrete, and that he might have been knocked unconscious by the fall. She lifted his head. The bridge of his nose was bleeding and might be broken, and there was a bad bruise on the forehead just above one eye. There was also a wound at the back of his head at the top of the spinal column, where the hard edge of the Scotch hand had struck him. It occurred to her that Alan might be dead.

It was cool in the dairy, and the quarry tiles on which she was kneeling were cold; she began to shiver. Her lips trembled. If she were to open her mouth, she might start to scream and be unable to stop. She must take control;

she must do something. She reached out for Alan's wrist to feel the pulse, but of course one can never find a pulse when one needs to do so. She turned him gently on his back. He did not respond; his eyes were open; she could not look at those eyes. She opened the front of his shirt, and put her hand on his chest to find the heart and feel it beat. Her hand was cooler than his skin; someone so warm could not be dead. She moved her hand over his chest. Her fingers seemed of their own accord to find a nipple and hold it, squeezing it between two fingers. Her coldness left her, and was succeeded by a burning flush. Her fingers squeezed and caressed the nipple. Would she feel it stiffen, would her touch bring it back to life? A part of her, a detached observing part, discovered that she was still shaking, but no longer from cold or fear. She must not look at his face. She moved her fingers downwards from the nipple, her whole hand down the skin of his chest to the stomach, to the navel then on further down, pushing under the waistband of his jeans, but she found no life. She lay on him, Susan on top of Alan, pressing her body against his, warming and kissing him, thrusting her tongue between his lips, breathing her own life into him, forcing it in, but the blank eyes stared back at her own closed eyes, and there was no life. Then Susan stood up, shook herself, and went back inside the house to tell Janet that she had killed Alan.

Janet said, 'We'll have to get rid of him.'
She did not wish to spend too long in the dairy because Butch had been left in the living-room play-area, and one never knew when he might discover that its ramparts could be pushed aside. In the nine months of his life so far she and Susan had worked out a way of coping with most emergencies which never involved leaving Butch unobserved, and she did not intend to start making exceptions.
'Bury him?' Janet shook her head. 'What then?'

'Give me time.'

The girls had not for a moment considered calling the police. Whether Alan's death was murder or manslaughter was irrelevant. Susan had not intended to kill him, but she had done so, and if it were discovered she would be punished by a term of imprisonment of whatever length the law might determine. Since imprisonment of any length of time would mean that the girls would be separated, and that Susan in particular would be separated from Butch, discovery would have to be prevented. Luckily, if Alan were to be believed, nobody knew of his intention to visit them.

'Cut him up?'

'Why?'

'I don't know. People do.'

'I don't see the point.'

'I suppose the waste-disposal unit wouldn't . . .?'

'It won't take large bones.' Janet looked down at Alan's body. She had liked him. They had walked together by the canal at Sykehouse, and joined in the militant choruses of the Jolly Cleggswood Boys, and shared a sleeping-bag. *"It's not a matter of whom you fuck; it's whom you love,"* and her mother had hit her. It was Susan she loved, Susan and Butch, who might even now be pushing at the padded boxes of the play-area as a preparation to crawling towards the fire. 'Septic tank,' she said.

They would not have to cut Alan up in order to put him in the septic tank which was quite large enough to take a body. The concrete slabs which covered it were not too heavy to be lifted and replaced. He would decompose there, all but the bones. There would be a stench, of course, but the septic tank always was niffy in summer, and there would be nobody to smell it but the girls themselves and Mrs Marshall. The bacteria of the septic tank ate up faeces and kitchen sludge flushed from the waste-disposal unit, and would in time eat up Alan.

It seemed the best course. They must not rush into it; they must consider it from all angles. First, the deed must not be done in daylight. There was a right of way running past the girls' house down to the road in the valley; it was used occasionally by ramblers, and sometimes by people on horses, and sometimes by villagers on a Sunday walk. In the early days of their occupancy, while the house was being restored and the garden taking shape, villagers had often walked by to look over the fence, but now that the girls were a known quantity, passing villagers were infrequent – yet they might still pass, even on a cold Sunday in March, and the ways of ramblers were unpredictable.

The church bell stopped its tolling; the bell-ringers themselves did not always stay for the service, in which case the congregation would not reach double figures. Although Alan must not be placed in the septic tank by daylight, the concrete slabs could be moved by Susan at tea-time under the pretence of gardening. They would be difficult to move in the dark. Even in daylight access to the septic tank required the negotiation of berberis and rugosa, both heavily thorned, and nettles were rife all round it. Trying to get in and move the slabs in the dark was likely to end in one of the girls' joining Alan among the sludge. Getting them back in place after they had put him in would be hard enough. The girls would have to use a torch, which was itself a risk, since lights in the house could be seen down in the village, and Mrs Hapgood of Pear Tree Cottage was always one to take an interest. 'Visitors last night,' she would say (Jake and Edna to dinner) or, 'Did you know you left your attic light on?' However, a torch pointed firmly downwards and masked by shrubs would make a very small glimmer seen only fitfully and might even be taken for fireflies.

Then there was the question of *rigor mortis*. At the age of sixteen Janet had read her way completely through the detective stories of Dorothy Sayers, the whole *oeuvre*, the property of an emancipated aunt. Details of the plot of *The Unpleasantness at the Bellona Club* began hazily to return to her. There had been an old gentleman, a retired colonel or general, who had been murdered and his body kept warm by a blazing fire in the Smoking Room, which had

85

delayed the onset of *rigor*. Members of the Club had thought him asleep behind *The Morning Post*, but he had been dead; Lord Peter Wimsey had solved it after some agony of mind, and the murderer had done the decent thing in the Library. In Miss Sayers' story it was the time of death which was important. With Alan the time of death would not be a problem, since the girls intended that his body should never be discovered, but *rigor mortis* would make getting him into the septic tank much more difficult than if the body were still limp. Undertakers were said sometimes to have to break the knees of corpses in order to get them downstairs. How soon would *rigor* set in? The girls consulted *The Readers' Digest Illustrated Medical Encylopaedia*, which informed them that it would be a few hours after death. How many hours were a few? Alan had died not long before eleven a.m.: it would be dark at six. They carried him from the dairy to the living-room, set him in an armchair by the fire, and put on more logs. Susan said, 'If he's not dead after all, the warmth of the fire might revive him,' but this was only self-delusion disguised as hope. They had put a mirror to Alan's mouth; they had tried everything. 'Oh God!' Janet said. 'Teeth!'

'What about them?'

'Identification.'

'You said he'd decompose.'

'The bones won't. Or the teeth. The bones don't matter. If they were ever found, he could be anyone, put in there while we were away; there's no proof. But the teeth would identify him.'

'But he's not going to be found.'

'One of us might die or get ill. We might have to sell the house. If the new people found a skeleton in the septic tank, there'd be an investigation.'

They looked at Alan, sitting there as agreeable as always in the armchair by the fire. A spark had landed without their noticing it on a leg of his jeans and burned a small hole. If *rigor* had set in already, also unnoticed, they would be unable to open his mouth; the jaws would be clamped together. It had not set in. Gently Susan parted

86

the lips and teeth, and held the jaws open for Janet to look. There were five fillings of tarnished silver. No bridgework; he was too young for it.

She wedged his jaws open with advertising material from *The Sunday Times Colour Supplement*. 'How many do we have to get rid of?'

'More than five, or they'd guess those were the ones.'

'All of them?'

'No, that would look deliberate.'

'Of course it would. It *is* deliberate.' Susan was beginning to feel sick, and used anger to mask it.

'Don't snap at me, Sukie.'

What did Jan think she was at? There were bruises already on Alan's face from the fall. Were they now to attack his teeth with some blunt instrument? It was no good. They had no experience in this sort of thing. It would all go wrong. 'We're not dentists. Whatever we do is going to look deliberate. Smashing them with a hammer. Anything. It's all deliberate.'

'Pliers.'

'Oh! . . . Yes. Sorry. Will there be blood?'

'Bound to be some. We'll take him into the kitchen, and prop him up against the sink. I expect there's less blood when you're dead. I mean, it's not circulating any more, is it? We'd better do it soon in case keeping him warm doesn't work.' Butch began to make the noise which was not crying but indicated that if lunch were not ready soon there might be trouble. 'I'll look for the pliers. You'd better give Butch something to eat.'

Susan chopped some cheese small and heated creamed rice over hot water while Janet searched the shed for pliers. When found they seemed neither oily nor rusty, but she cleaned them nevertheless with wire wool, washed them in hot water and disinfectant, dried them with paper towels, and laid them out on a clean J-cloth. Then she put on rubber gloves. There was no need for any of this, since Alan was dead, but it seemed more respectful. They discovered that they could not prop Alan over the sink, keep his mouth open, and work inside it,

87

so they sat him in a kitchen chair with his head back as if he were at the hairdresser's being shampooed, and extracted eight teeth. There was very little blood. Susan said, 'At least he doesn't need a local anaesthetic,' and her eyes filled with tears.

It was clear to Janet that Susan was in a very up-and-down state, and would have been better in bed with as much Sleep Compleat as it was safe to take, but there was still too much for both of them to do. She said, 'Let's get him back to the fire. We're going to have to undress him and burn his clothes. We'd better do that now, just in case.'

'Won't he get cold?'

'We shan't be able to do it if he stiffens up.'

'We could cut them off him.'

That was better. Susan was beginning to think practically. As long as one could reduce Alan's death and the manner of it to the dimensions of a problem, one could cope. Later there would be lying awake, tears and shuddering, anxiety and useless regret. Guilt was bound to damage them both, what they had done and were to do was bound to lurk in their waking memories, re-emerging swollen and distorted in nightmares, but as long as they remained together they could bear it and survive it. 'Right!' Jan said, 'Let's put him back in the chair. It's time for Butch's nap.'

Butch held out one arm and made play-with-me noises to Alan as the girls carried him back into the living-room. Butch was over-excited; it would be difficult getting him off to sleep, requiring a flow of gentle chat and the manipulation of mobiles. Janet left Susan to do it, put the eight teeth in a paper bag, and went out to the woods with a trowel to bury them. They would be safe enough there, requiring only a small hole; there would be no freshly turned pile of earth over a new grave to cry murder. Anyone might go into the woods with a trowel now that the bluebells were already showing green. Janet dug a small hole, put in the bag of teeth, covered it with earth, and stamped the earth flat. Later that night the teeth were dug up by a fox, some crunched and the rest dispersed: they were safe from discovery and identification.

At tea-time Susan went out to move the slabs. Shortly afterwards the rain began again. At five o'clock they discovered that the fire had not worked, or anyway not enough; Alan had stiffened in a sitting position. Butch had his evening meal, was bathed, and put to bed. The dark came slowly. Although it was Sunday, no roast had been put into the oven. The girls would have something cold afterwards if they felt like it.

At eight o'clock Janet said, 'Well?'

Susan said, 'It's easy for you to be calm. You didn't kill him.'

'I'm not calm, Sue.'

'Sorry.'

They listened. No sound from Butch upstairs in his cot. He would be well asleep by this time, and unlikely to wake before three a.m. They cut Alan out of his clothes with kitchen scissors, and put the guard in front of the fire against sparks. The rain was still pelting down; they would need to wear their duffel coats and wellies, which would make them clumsy. Alan's eyes were wide open. Susan tried to pull down the lids with her thumb, but they would not pull. They discovered that the torch had been left in the van, and Susan had to go out for it; it was one of those long strong rubber torches, and gave a good light. By a quarter to nine they were ready. It was surprisingly easy to lift and carry Alan in a sitting position; they put their arms beneath his bum and made a cradle. They carried him out into the dark and rain of the garden like a hero being chaired by team-mates, the light from the torch in Janet's hand bobbing down steps and over grass. They reached the shrubbery. 'This is the difficult bit,' Susan said.

She had chosen a route between potentilla and cotoneaster, avoiding the thorny shrubs. The cotoneaster had originally been intended to grow laterally to cover and disguise the slabs over the tank, but had chosen an upright habit instead, which was just as well under the circumstances. Even so its foliage was dense. The girls were still carrying Alan between them; he could not be carried in any other way, stiff as he was. Consequently they had to enter the shrubbery sideways. Susan took the torch. 'I'll go first. I know the way.' She had left the slabs on the other side of the tank where they would not be fallen over. What had now to be done was that Susan, at one end of the septic tank, remained where she was while Janet moved round at a ninety-degree angle to the other end. Unfortunately there was forsythia in the way. Susan could not have anticipated that Alan would be carried rigid, sitting on their linked arms. She had imagined him limp in a fireman's lift.

The torch waved as if signalling to Germans. They would have to set Alan down among the nettles while Janet got into place; it would not matter about his being wet and muddy when one considered where he was going anyway, nor would he be troubled by the stings of nettles. The girls struggled to get him into a position from which he could be lifted again. Twigs reached out at them from the dark, striking at their faces, catching in their hair, but if they were to protect themselves with the hoods of their duffel coats, they would not be able to see at all. Susan struck angrily at a twig, the beam of the torch made a track in the night sky, and something in the forsythia broke. 'Susan!' The shrubbery would look tomorrow as if wild beasts had been fighting in it, and must not. 'Nothing out of the ordinary,' Janet had said. 'Nobody knows he's been here, and nobody must know. It's the only way.' Yet if Susan were not to be lacerated, the shrubbery must be; marks on her were as little to be desired as marks on it. 'Easy, Sukie!' They managed to set Alan down, still in the sitting position, tilted against Susan's legs. She shone the torch on him, and his white face looked up at her, eyes staring, the bruises livid, hair plastered over his forehead by the rain. He seemed to be asking, 'Why?' Inside the house the telephone began to ring. She knew at once that the call was for Alan. He had told someone in London that he would be visiting the girls on his way, and when he had not arrived, the someone had phoned. Susan dropped the torch, and it fell into the septic tank.

'It's the phone.' There was an extension bell on the wall of the house, and the north-west wind blew down the garden. The ringing could be clearly heard. 'Who can it be?'

'How the hell do I know? It could be anyone. A wrong number. Let it ring.'

'It's for him. Somebody knows he's visiting us. We'll have to get him back in the house.'

'He can't answer it, Sukie. He's dead.'

'I dropped the torch.'

'I know.' The telephone stopped ringing.

Clouds obscured the moon. The girls looked into the septic tank and saw a light below them in the murk. The torch had fallen on its side. Sludge had broken its fall, and into that sludge it had sunk some way. One of them had only to reach in, and pull it out.

'When you took the slabs off this afternoon, what was in there?' In spite of the rain and the wind, there was a smell of ordure from the tank.

'Sludge. Stuff floating. Awful.'

'Shit?'

'Of course there was shit. Gunge and shit. You can smell it.'

'Don't bother about the torch, then. Let it lie. We'll manage in the dark.'

It was better in the dark, more difficult but better; Susan could not see Alan's face. They lifted him between them and managed to get him into the tank. It had not occurred to the girls that the displacement would cause the tank to overflow. Janet said, 'You'll have to come back in the morning early, and dig over the ground.' That would not arouse interest or suspicion; it would have been done anyway to get rid of the nettles before they became uncontrollable. Alan had turned over when they put him in, and floated face downwards in the filth as if reaching out

91

for the torch, his white bum glinting in the dark. *"I'm not calm, Sue."* Susan imagined Janet's face, closed against all emotion, expressing only the determination to hold the two of them together and get the job done. The concrete slabs, placed so carefully to one side, had become fouled by the overflow and slippery. With difficulty the girls managed to replace them. Susan said, 'I hope you don't mind; I'd like to say the Lord's Prayer. There ought to be something.' They stood together in the dark and rain amid shit and sludge, and said the Lord's Prayer together, and the wind blew the words down the valley. As they returned to the house, the telephone began to ring again.

Susan answered. It was Mrs Marshall, phoning from the public box in the village.

'Did you phone before? Not long ago?'

'No reply. I was worried. You should have been in on a Sunday, and there's a downstairs light on.' The curtains were drawn in the living-room, but the village knew there was a downstairs light on. 'Mrs Hapgood says there was flashlights in your garden waving about. Sent her Trevor over to my caravan. There's been a lot of vandalism. Hell's Angels in Kineton; I put my coat on, and came out to the box. You didn't answer. I got worried. Thought I'd better tell the police.'

A chill; it was like paralysis. 'And did you tell the police?' Jan was staring at her. 'What did you say?'

'Sunday isn't it? Duncan does his courting.' There were always several scandals going at once in the village, the details passed about like presents. The policeman was a newcomer from the north, a conscientious lad with butter-coloured hair. His van was often to be seen parked in a lay-by on the Stratford road of a Sunday night with sounds of pleasurable commotion coming from the back. 'Might have been a wrong number. Tried again. Where were you?'

Susan discovered that she could not think how to reply. Where were they? What had they been doing? However, the paralysis had left her. Although she could not speak, she could turn and look at Jan.

92

'Are you there, Susan?'

'Mrs Marshall wants to know what we were doing in the garden. Mrs Hapgood saw lights flashing, and sent her Trevor.'

'What?'

'Just talking to Janet.'

Janet said calmly, being Janet, being always calm, although she was not calm, only maintaining an appearance of calmness so that there should be nothing out of the ordinary, said calmly, 'Tell her about the fox. We thought it might be after the chickens.'

'We thought a fox might be after the chickens.'

'What?'

'Tell her about the noise the chickens were making, so we had to go out and see what was the matter.'

'The chickens were making a noise, so we went out to see what the matter was.'

'Tell her we thought there might be a hole in the wire.'

'We thought there might be a hole in the wire. We thought a fox might have got in. We thought it might be after the chickens. They were making such a noise, we went to see. It was rainy and very windy. We had to take a torch with us. We heard you ring.' Jan was making wind-it-up motions with one hand. 'That's all it was. Nothing out of the ordinary. I'm sorry it alarmed Mrs Hapgood. Would you tell her? Goodnight, Mrs Marshall. Thank you so much for phoning.'

They were wet. They were filthy and smelly. They rinsed their hands in disinfectant in case the concrete slabs should have grazed them. They ran a hot bath with rosemary bath essence, and got in it together. They decided that they were hungry after all, and would not be satisfied with cold. There was no time to cook the Sunday joint, but they opened tins of baked beans, made cocoa, fried eggs and bacon, even fried bread which is known to be the worst thing and would put on pounds as well as cholesterol. They made the most enormous fry-up and ate it by the fire.

Then they burned Alan's clothes, ground up the

93

buttons in the waste-disposal unit, and dumped the belt-buckle with egg-shells and bacon rinds in the garbage sack. Then they went to bed.

8

THE FLOWER SHOW

Spring was cold and late that year. Potatoes and broad beans were planted later than usual, and the first sowing of peas never came up. Tomato plants in the conservatory had to be protected at night against frost by a paraffin heater. Peppers and aubergines remained in peat pots on the kitchen window, and grew leggy. Early in April the snow returned, and the girls were cut off from the village for two days.

Alan was slow in decomposing. Bubbles burst, one must assume, in the septic tank. Little circles of stench rose from it, and were blown away by the north wind. Susan furtively poured yeast from the wine-making cupboard between the concrete slabs, hoping to speed the process. The girls moved the two bee-hives to another part of the garden. Nobody looked beneath the slabs.

It still was not real to them. Provided that his body could be prevented from returning to inconvenience or distress them, Alan was not really dead. They were children, playing at concealing a murder as they played at self-sufficiency. They were amateurs in a game of which the only professionals are the army and the secret police. Individuals, however careful and ingenious, do not win at such a game. The mass-murderer Haigh used a bath of acid. The mass-murderer Nilsen cut up the bodies of his victims, boiled them in pots on the gas-stove, and flushed their cooked flesh down the w.c. Hans Haarmann, the butcher of Hanover, made succulent mince and sausages of the young boys whom he picked up at the railway station, and sold them in his shop. All were in time found out and brought to trial. Should the girls have sent Alan out to mail-order customers as *confit* or terrine, or made meat-pies of him like Mrs Lovett? They never thought of it, could not have done it. They wanted him out of sight, out of mind, forgotten; they wanted him never to have lived; they wanted Butch, like Jesus Christ, never to have had a mortal father. While the weather remained cold, it seemed as if they had their wish.

So it went throughout April. Even in early May there was frost on the lawn and little sun. Blackthorn bloomed with the promise of sloes, but hawthorn and crab held back and the ash was still bare of leaves. Mrs Marshall's fingers had never continued arthritic so late in the year. The doctor changed her pills, but the new ones were worse than the old, and went straight to her stomach. There were no enquiries from the north or from any friends who might have been expecting Alan in London; perhaps there were no such friends. He had told Janet that he had taken off without warning; he would have kept his intention to visit the girls a secret, perhaps not even acknowledging it to himself in case he should change his mind. He would have been missed by now by his parents and by Bob, his partner. They would have expected his return, wondered and worried, finally reported his absence to the police. 'He just went off one day, said he was going to London on a visit, never told us when he'd be back; we've not seen him since; it's been weeks.' Weeks, months, March until May, and still no word from him. He would have been entered on the police files as a Missing Person, but there were so many young men and young women and children too, in the seventies as now, who went missing every year, far too many for the police to concern themselves in cases where there was no positive evidence of any more than discontent in those who chose to go. They would turn up again or they would not; adrift in the cities they would find charitable agencies to look after them.

96

What had they done, Alan's parents and his partner, when Alan did not return, and the police had no information and no help for them? His partner would be worried about the business as well as for Alan himself. Had he kept Alan's place open, or was he already training a successor? They had been friends as well as partners. The parents would blame him for Alan's itchy feet, and he would feel guilt as well as bereavement. And the parents themselves? Did his mother still wait every morning for the postman while the father lay obstinately in bed, having already completed the emotional journey from vexation through anxiety to despair? Alan had been an only child; his parents would not easily have accepted the loss. Had they written to hospitals, travelled to London themselves, lodging in cheap bed-and-breakfast places to spin out the money, making the rounds of Centre Point, the Samaritans, the Salvation Army, lingering among the homeless under the arches, riding round and round the Inner Circle hoping to happen on him? For most of the time the girls tried to block out such questions, and for most of the time succeeded, assisted by the unseasonable cold.

Then the weather turned warmer, and the tank began to stink. The girls had expected a stench, but had thought it would be like the one to which they were already accustomed, only stronger. This was different, the sickly stench of rotting meat, impossible to confuse with the homely familiar country stench of a septic tank in summer.

Although the septic tank had been built in 1967, the principles of its construction predated the government's Revised Building Regulations of 1965. Beneath the concrete slabs was only an open box of brick, with a pipe at the top to let in the sewage, the solid elements of which sank to the bottom where there was another pipe by which the liquids drained away into sub-soil. The solids, when they had been sufficiently clawed and chewed by bacteria, would become small enough to drain away also as a cloudiness in the liquid. Nowadays there would be a further tank containing sharp gravel as a filtering element, nowadays the input pipe would be porous and laid over gravel, nowadays the tank itself might be one of those huge pre-formed porous bottles one sees being carried on the backs of lorries (usually when one is travelling behind them uphill), which are sunk directly into the soil and which contain all the necessary filters and chemicals to do the work. Such a bottle might have digested Alan with no great difficulty, nor any eructation of wind and stink, but the primitive construction of the girls' septic tank was not up to such a task. Alan was a solid far larger than any in its experience. It would take time to digest him. Meanwhile he stank.

Winds from the north and east would blow the stench down the valley, to be dissipated long before it reached any other human habitation. Winds from the south and west blew it back towards the house in gusts, and on those days all the doors and windows were closed, Butch taken early to the shop, and the girls prayed that no one from the Midlands Electricity Board would come to read the meter. When there was no wind at all, the stench lay about the lower reaches of the garden like a miasma, thick and invisible, so that one might blunder into it unknowingly and feel it fill one's lungs with oily poison which persisted long after one had blundered quickly out again. Luckily the chickens (and now the bees) were on the north side of the house, the vegetable garden to the east, but even so Susan took to working in dark glasses and with a scarf covering her mouth and nose. As for the dairy, it was not entered except upon necessity, and the door kept firmly closed.

With the stench there came a plague of flies, mostly blowflies, but also house flies, horse flies, soldier flies and midges. The girls hung flypapers in the kitchen, and set pots of basil on window-sills. The flypapers caught in their hair, and house flies settled on the basil, and left specks on the leaves. They sat together in the conservatory after Butch had been put to bed, with a block of Vapona insecticide on every joist, and looked down at the shrubbery, and it seemed to them both that there was a haze of flies rising from the septic tank, up through the concrete blocks, up past even the tallest shrubs, a spiral of flies rising like the souls of the dead on the Last Day.

Mrs Marshall came in on Wednesdays to help with the cleaning. That had not been a problem during the first weeks of unseasonable weather. The girls discussed ways to put her off, but could think of none which was practical; any emergency would bring Mrs Marshall up all the quicker to deal with it. 'Nothing out of the ordinary' must still be their guiding principle. Mrs Marshall enjoyed her day at the girls' house, particularly in summer, and anything which kept her away would be remembered and questioned. On the first Wednesday after the stench began, the wind, though slight, was from the east and the flowers she chose for her arrangements were all from the cottage-garden outside the kitchen; she never went near the shrubbery. Butch was having a picnic lunch with Janet at the shop, but for Mrs Marshall Susan made a mousse of salmon and cucumber, and they lingered over it with cider and curd cheese and wholemeal bread until Mrs Marshall said, 'Oh God! Is that the time? I must get on,' and the danger of exploration and explanation was passed, and that was the first Wednesday.

On the second Wednesday Susan was in the shop and there was no wind. Janet was in the conservatory with Butch; she would be able to keep an eye on the shrubbery and to head off Mrs Marshall if she were to come through for flowers. The shank of the morning had passed with no more incident than the usual minor damage to the vacuum cleaner, and lunch had passed. It had been soup, which Butch could share; Mrs Marshall always enjoyed the girls' soups, particularly those containing lovage. There were only ninety minutes to go, but the flower-arrangements had not yet been created, and they were the danger. The windows of the conservatory were open, because heat built up in there during a sunny afternoon, causing the tomato plants to wilt. From time to time, Janet breathed deeply to test the air, but there was only the warm smell of the tomato foliage, and perhaps a hint of

99

sourness from Butch whom she did not dare take upstairs to change.

'Shall we put you down for Dauntsey's?' The books agreed that every opportunity must be taken to engage the baby in conversation. 'That would please your grandfather. My dad would be tickled pink, Butchles, if we put you down for his old school.' No concept would be too complicated for the baby at this stage. Conversation itself was the object, a continuous dialogue, even though the sounds made by either side were incomprehensible to the other. 'Oh, you'd prefer Eton, would you? Snobby little bugger!' Thus would the baby become accustomed to the concept of speech as an easy and natural means of communication between human beings. 'Well, you'll have to start at the village school anyway. We'll put you down for that, shall we?' Conversation must be made directly to the baby and with eye-contact. He would not profit to the same extent from listening to the girls talking to each other, because that would exclude him. 'Oh God! Oh God, God!' Mrs Marshall had just appeared in the lower garden, having reached it by way of the rockery, and was standing stock still, an expression of shock apparent even in her back and shoulders.

Mrs Marshall turned, shrugged her shoulders towards Janet in the conservatory, and spread her hands. Was that it? Would she now gather whatever flowers she needed, and ask no questions, regarding the septic tank as not being part of the house and therefore not within her province? Oh God, let that be it! Mrs Marshall was a woman of idiosyncratic ways and strong beliefs. Let that be it. She began to walk up from the garden towards the conservatory. That was not it. She would ask questions and must be given answers.

'Who've you got in there?'

Who, not *what*: the shock was very great. It was as if a whole series of defences had been swept aside. Janet pasted a smile carefully on her face from the inside. No one would actually ask 'who?' and mean it. Mrs Marshall

100

was making a joke, and must be answered by a joke. 'Butch's dad?'

'Thought that might be it.'

Away went the next series, the palisades, the moat, the outer wall of the castle itself. However, the most likely interpretation remained a joke, which, once begun and answered in the same vein, must now be continued. Janet did not know how to continue it, so she remained silent, and Mrs Marshall continued.

'Rotting meat, that smell. Used to get it round the butcher's, round the back, when I was a girl. Comes in a van these days, and straight into the cold room, but the old butcher, he'd kill his own. Slaughter a pig for you any time. Hang it up, cut its throat. Bloody object'd scream for hours and then die. Hear it all over the village. Hear it three mile away. Butch's dad, eh? You didn't want him hanging round, I suppose. Come to make trouble, did he?'

It was not a joke. Mrs Marshall knew. There was no point in lying. Ought she to run to the telephone, and tell Susan to get into the van, drive and keep driving? There was a shot-gun upstairs, kept for rabbits and seldom used, but even if she were able to do it, Janet had not the stomach to shoot Mrs Marshall and put her also in the septic tank, nor would there be room for her. And everyone knew Mrs Marshall came to the girls on Wednesdays.

'You'd better sit down before you fall.'

Janet said, 'Nobody meant to kill him. It was an accident.'

'Susan?'

'Yes.'

Mrs Marshall clicked her tongue.

'Impulsive.'

'Instinctive. He said something, and she hit him. She didn't mean it.'

'Period due, I expect.'

'Well . . . yes.' Janet was surprised. Susan's period

101

had, in fact, come on early, the day after Alan's death, but she had not considered the connection.

'Always edgy, that one, a day or two before. Sweet as pie the week after.'

'What are you going to do?'

'About him? Same as you. Wait. Nothing else *to* do. Won't last forever. Anyone asks questions, you'd better say some of that pâté of yours went bad, and hope the Public Health Officer doesn't get to hear of it.' A fly settled on Mrs Marshall's bare forearm and she swatted it vigorously; the warmer weather had taken care of her arthritis as it always did. 'Bloody objects! Well, I better get on. I've got my flowers to do.'

Although the theory was that the cloudy liquid of the septic tank drained into the sub-soil, to be thoroughly filtered before joining the water-table of the West Midlands, the fact was a little more complicated owing to the situation of the girls' house and garden halfway down a hill. The garden had been the farmyard when the house had been a farm. It had been terraced, with paved patio and cottage garden to one side of the house, the vegetable garden beyond the drive, the old bakehouse adapted to the dairy, the outside privy to a rockery, only the back wall of the pig-sty remaining for cordons of apples and peach to grow against – oh, it had all been thoroughly renovated with a maximum use of existing materials and features. A terrace of lawn between the dairy and conservatory had been supported by a wall of local stone against which roses had been trained, and below it there was a further lawn with a pool, beds of heathers, water garden and weeping pear which led down to the shrubbery (with septic tank), and beyond that a hedge, beyond which – that was it; that was the problem – beyond the hedge a steep drop to a small stream. This stream began as a spring just below the edge of the woods, entered the girls' garden from the east, was

102

confined in a cement channel to feed the pool, left it again by way of a series of waterfalls, and found its way back to its original bed, running along the whole bottom edge of the garden, then turned at a right angle and proceeded on through fields until it disappeared, a mile from the house, into a culvert under the road. Presumably it emerged at some point from this culvert and ran on, as is the way of water, but the girls had never asked where or whither.

You are with me, I think; you may already be ahead of me. What, viewed objectively, was merely the steep slope of the bank of the stream at the bottom of the garden, viewed another way might be considered as more like an earth wall beyond the brick wall of the septic tank. It was thick – about two and a half metres – but the girls had observed that the bank on their side always seemed damp, and nettles grew particularly lushly there. They had observed more than this, if the truth is to be told; they had sometimes observed, in winter when the nettles had died back, moisture trickling from the bank, not in rivulets, but in what was least a profuse perspiration. They had not spoken of this to others, since only cattle ever drank from the stream, but they had wondered about it. They wondered particularly about it now.

Was Alan a health hazard? They could not continue to conceal him if that were so. Only cattle drank, but cows and sheep, although not human, were living beings and the livelihood of humans. Vague recollections came to Susan – were they from the Bible? from history lessons at school? a novel from the days when she read novels? – of a conquered people who had filled their wells with corpses so as to spread pestilence among their conquerors. She was waking early these days, and finding it difficult to go back to sleep. She told herself that it was the early daylight, that she always woke early in the summer, but the muscles of her jaws would be clenched and while sleeping she ground her teeth. She would lie awake, keeping as motionless as she could so as not to wake Jan, and at these times such recollections came to her. Usually

103

Jan would be awake also, lying still so as not to wake Susan, forcing her mind to consider only the familiar routines of the coming day. Butch never woke early. He seemed happy these days to sleep the whole night through and take a couple of naps during the day as well.

On June 5th, the morning of Butch's first birthday, Susan woke from a dream of trying to push away the concrete blocks over her head. They had planned nothing special for Butch that day, since he was not of an age to appreciate anything more sophisticated than a koala bear with nylon fur, but had decided to go out themselves for a meal, leaving Mrs Marshall to babysit. Susan looked at her watch. A quarter to five. She could not lie awake for three hours or so; it was not in her to do so this morning. She must do something. She would follow the stream; if it were poisoned, she might be able to tell. Then she would go to the police and confess, and it would all be over, and somehow Jan would survive. They would put her in prison, but perhaps not for long; in any case, a life sentence was never really for life. In time she would emerge, and find her way back, purged, and Butch would be a young man by then, and she would say, very simply, 'Butch, I am your other mother,' and they would both cry, and Jan would cry, and so would Mrs Marshall, and maybe Jake and Edna, and it would all be beautiful.

She got quietly out of bed, but heard Jan stir 'Just going to say "Happy Birthday" to Butch, and then I thought I'd go for a bit of a walk.'

'What time is it?'

'Early. Go back to sleep, love. I'm only going for a walk. It's a special day. I wanted to do something special.'

'I thought we were going out to dinner.'

'Something else. Different. It's the best time of the morning. I thought I'd walk through the dew.'

'Christ!'

'Don't worry. I'll say "Happy Birthday" very quietly. I shan't wake him.'

'Do you want me to come with you?'

'Don't fuss. Go back to sleep.'

104

Rabbits were feeding up the hill at the edge of the wood. The click of the front gate startled them, and they ran. Susan followed the right of way in the field on the edge of the garden. If she had really wanted to walk through the dew, she had her wish; the dew was abundant, and the early-morning mist rose from it, and swirled about her wellies. She could see that further down in the valley the mist was deeper, almost to the height of the hedges.

The air was fresh and invigorating at first, then became foul as she drew level with the shrubbery, then gradually cleared again. The stream ran between two fields, divided from one by a hedge, from the other by a wire-and-post fence. Susan had determined that as soon as she could no longer smell the stench of the septic tank, she would examine the stream. She would look closely along the banks for dead mammals or birds, and she had brought an empty jam-jar to collect a sample of the water which she would send for analysis – she was not sure where; she would have to ask. She climbed through the wire of the fence, and approached the stream. It was always overgrown in summer; seeds washed down from the garden, blown by winds, carried by birds, had colonised the stream with mimulus, bugle and *primula florindae* the giant cowslip, and the girls themselves had thrown into it the rhizomes of irises surplus to requirements after division, though most of those were up near the shrubbery. Here, lower down, there were patches of bugle on the lower bank, and mimulus had grown in the bed of the stream itself, and had already broken into flowers of bright yellow blotched with red. Was it growing more thickly than usual? Yes, it was; it covered the water. There was a forest of mimulus, fighting on equal terms the nettles and thistles, dock and cow parsley indigenous to the stream, and the giant cowslips had grown as tall as wheat.

But was all this a sign of health or pestilence? Whichever it was, there was the danger that if vegetation grew too lushly in the stream, Mr Heavitree who farmed the fields on both sides would be up to clear it, the whole length of it from the shrubbery down, and questions would be asked about the stench of decay from the septic tank. 'Some pâté went bad.' The roots of the mumulus were so matted that one could not get through them to the water to fill a jam-jar. Would anyone believe that a few pounds of pigs' liver and belly of pork could do so much?

Susan bent low into the mimulus, wrenching the stems and roots apart, her rump protruding from the mass of flowers. A blackbird chattered angrily in the hedge above her. There was a sound at the bottom of the field from the gate connecting it to the field below. *'Hup!'* She dropped the top of the jam-jar, scrabbled in vegetation for it, stood up quickly and turned to find out who else was in the field so early in the morning. She was just in time to see, rising out of the mist like Pegasus to leap the hedge, a white horse and a man riding it.

The horse trotted towards her. The mist came up to its fetlocks so that it appeared to be trotting through cloud. The rider was a man in early middle age, bareheaded with dark curly hair and a face which had been much in the open air. He wore riding breeches, and a tweed jacket over a polo-neck sweater. It was not farmers' gear; he would be a guest at the Manor. 'Shouldn't have done that,' he said.

'Sorry?' She was still holding the jam-jar, but there seemed to be nowhere to put it. Was he accusing her? 'Shouldn't have done that'? She had done nothing but try to take some water from the stream. He could not know her reason for wanting it.

'Suddenly discovered that I didn't feel like getting off and leading her through the gate. Seemed mean somehow, at this hour of the morning.'

'Oh! . . . ' "Her"? Of course; the horse was a mare. They had jumped the hedge. 'No, you shouldn't. Not without a crash-helmet.'

'Might have been wire. Wasn't, but there might have been. You look like Ruth, knee-high amid the alien corn.

Except that it's flowers in your case. Is it like mushrooms? Do you have to get up this early to pick them?'

'They're mimulus. They get washed down from our garden, and grow in the stream.'

'Fine crop.' He lifted his head, and sniffed the air. 'Well manured. What have you got up there, an abbatoir?'

No man from the MEB had called, no telephone engineer, no land-rover of hunters with shot-guns licensed to shoot rabbits and wood-pigeon, no mole-catcher, no maintenance-engineer for the oil-heater, no unexpected delivery by British Road Services or Securicor; even Mr Heavitree, although he had harrowed and ferti-lised the fields, had not come within sniffing distance. Only Mrs Marshall had divined their secret, and she was close as the grave. And now, on the very morning when Susan herself had come out, responsibly, to make sure that Alan, decomposing, put no one else at risk, she, Susan, prepared to take the consequences if he did, to go voluntarily to the police and the Public Health Officer, on this very morning there came a stranger on a white horse, blundering over hedges without a crash-helmet, lifting his nose in the air to sniff out their secret: it was too much. She had turned pale, and then red, and could not speak. He was smiling down at her. His teeth were whiter than is usual in men and his eyes a clear grey beneath thick eyebrows.

'Some pâté went bad.'

He sniffed the air again, and the mare moved a front leg restlessly in the mist. He knew, of course.

'Shouldn't worry about it if I were you. Everything passes.'

'Eh?'

'Everything passes, including me. Good morning to you. You keep quiet about my jumping the hedge, and I'll keep quiet about your pâté.' He patted the mare on her neck, and she tossed her head and took a step forward.

'Wait!' He had already gone a little way from her, his back towards her. She could hardly run after him. There were three strands of wire between herself and the field. 'Who are you?'

He stopped the mare, and looked back at her. The mist seemed to grow thicker round him, swirling up from the grass in gusts, so that both horse and rider became for a moment almost insubstantial. 'Never know who you'll meet in the country. Piper at the gates of dawn, that sort of thing. Don't worry.' He turned away again, and set the mare to galloping across the field. 'Everything passes,' he shouted, and was lost to sight in the mist.

It occurred to Susan that, although the man had seemed very well able to sniff the scent of the septic tank, she herself had chosen this spot precisely because she was not able to smell it at all.

From that day the stench quickly diminished, and by the end of the month it had altogether gone, and the septic tank reverted to its usual stench in summer, which was expected if not particularly attractive, and had nothing to do with rotting flesh, or at least not in an undigested state. Susan chose to believe that the man on the white horse had been responsible for this, that he was Pan or some similar nature-god, and in support of this contention she pointed out that he was hairy, that he had appeared out of mist as the gods were said to do, had displayed a preternatural knowledge of what was amiss, and then put it to rights. Furthermore he had been riding a mare, which had associations of sexuality, Pan being one of the more sexually active gods, and anyway he had said he was Pan, as good as, quoting the chapter of *The Wind in the Willows* (a book he must have known Susan had read) in which the god actually appears.

Janet disagreed. She did not see that the encounter was of any great significance. Viewed objectively, nothing out of the ordinary had happened. A man out riding in the early morning (the best time of day for it) had caught a whiff of the septic tank, had been given Mrs Marshall's 'pâté' explanation, and been satisfied by it. As for the piper at the gates of dawn, a great many people have read *The Wind in the Willows*. Men liked to show off, in Janet's experience, and were not above making a mystery where there was none. And of course the stench had disappeared. It had had to disappear sometime; decomposing bodies did eventually complete the process of decomposition, and thereafter ceased to stink. She herself was surprised that it had taken so long.

These opposite interpretations of what may or may not have been a supernatural event illustrate the difference between the girls' ways of looking at life. It was a difference which, one might say, accounted in part for their having come together and remained together, but it was a dangerous difference none the less, and was later to cause them both distress.

Meanwhile the good days began again, and although Butch had, since his birthday, become something of a pest, that was only in the opinions of others, never of the girls who were delighted by his increased activity. Babies, the books said, grow fastest in the spring. Well, spring had been late this year, but it was with them now, and Butch grew apace both in size and in capability. There was no longer any doubt that he could walk; all that Marcel Marceau acting had been quite given up. It is true that he walked with his feet well apart like an old lady who has wet herself, and that he preferred to be within reach of support; indeed, without support he could take no more than three paces before falling over and beginning to yell. It is also true that he had not yet mastered sitting down from a standing position, and that if he required to sit he would have to remain where he was, holding onto a chair or box or window-seat, and yell for help. One way and another, Butch did a good deal of yelling in the month of June, 1976. He had also developed the habit of grabbing anything portable within his reach and either eating it or trying to take it apart or both. The girls continued to be enchanted by him. They spoke to him constantly of their plans for him and for each other.

They read to him, and told him the names of numbers and colours and how to cook a cassoulet. They listened to birdsong with him and showed him flowers. They bought him pop-up books, and when he tore out the pop-up insertions they congratulated him on his dexterity. They built towers of soft objects for him to knock over. Whatever he chose to do, they cuddled and congratulated him. Butch, when not actually yelling, would usually receive the girls' conversation in thoughtful silence, but sometimes he would talk to them in a sweetly flowing river of chat which may have been Tibetan, may even have been Welsh, may have been river-language itself; it had the chuckling gurgling quality of a river, and was both comforting and invigorating to the girls as rivers are to those who listen.

What are so unseasonable as the English seasons? By mid-June it had become clear that the delayed spring was to be followed by a drought, and all through July the grass withered and shallow-rooted plants grew sick. There were restrictions on the use of hoses, cars were not to be washed or lawns sprinkled, and the people of Britain were requested not to flush their w.c.s after each occasion of use, but to wait upon severe necessity. Luckily the spring which supplied the pool in the girls' garden did not dry up, so that the watering of vegetables and fruit-trees was able to continue, though it became burdensome when it had to be done by bucket and watering-can. The conservatory became a green cave in which the scent of ripening melons and tomatoes mingled, and grapes grew heavy on the vine, and grabbing by small fingers had to be actively discouraged. The shop prospered as passing trade snapped up the salads and cheeses, drank all the home-made ginger beer, and made a not-to-be-explained run upon broad beans. Even the lace went; anything with holes seemed cool to passing trade.

It was all done by work, hard work, and the girls, especially Susan, rejoiced in it, hoeing and watering and harvesting, gathering eggs and honey, cooking and sewing and selling. It was all for each other and for Butch, performed for much of the time in his presence, watched by him, interrupted by him, distracted by him. He could be taken freely into the garden now that the miasma of the septic tank had gone; even passers-by on the right of way would be welcomed, and there would be conversations over the fence. Janet tried to make herself believe that Alan had been dried out by the drought, baked, withered, desiccated, but of course it could not be that, since water did still drain into the septic tank from the house as baths were taken, faces and dishes washed, and Butch in particular was a great consumer of water.

'Oh God!' Susan said. 'The backs of my thighs do ache. I've got great lumpy muscles coming up all over. I must look like a parcel,' and Jan said, 'I like muscular women. Roll over, and I'll give you a massage.' Butch never interrupted such moments. It was one of his many virtues.

In bed next morning Jan said, 'Do you ever think about Alan?'

'Not really. I wonder about the people where he came from sometimes. His mother and dad, and that friend of his with the beard. What *they* feel. And about us if . . . I think about being found out. Often. I worry about that. But when I dream about it, then it's always me in the tank. The smell is always me. Flesh going bad, maggots; that's my flesh. Nightmares. Hair growing in the water, growing out of the top of the tank like weed; that's my hair. I don't think about Alan at all. He's just a blank.'

'I think about him.'

Susan felt a moment of jealousy, and moved a little apart.

'When he took his clothes off that time in the van, I thought he looked like a rabbit. He was a rabbit, in more ways than one.' Sue grunted. 'No, I don't mean that; I told you about that; he was no good at that. But he was so vulnerable. Eager to please, wanting to be liked. Rabbits. You look at them, specially the young ones, and

111

they look so appealing. They never hurt anyone. I mean, they do a lot of damage, but they don't know they're doing it. We'd shoot a rabbit if we saw one in the vegetable patch.' Jan stopped herself from adding 'at least you would', though it was always Susan who shot the rabbits. 'And we killed Alan as soon as he came onto *our* patch. Instinctive. That's what people do to rabbits – in the country anyway – shoot them, gas them, give them myxomatosis. But there are a lot of rabbits, and there was only one of him.'

'Don't.' Sue rolled over in the bed, put her arms around Jan, and hugged her.

'All right, I won't. We'll get up, and give his nibs his breakfast.'

But as Butch sat in his high chair attempting, with instruction and assistance, to feed himself from a plastic spoon, Susan looked at him carefully. The baby pudginess had begun to fall away, and Butch was beginning to look less like Winston Churchill and more like an ordinary human being. Was there a hint of rabbit? He struck out, and the spoon and its eggy contents went flying. No, he was all Jan; she was sure of that.

Janet said, 'You should have told me about the dreams.'

'They're better now, since the man on the horse.'

In the United States of America, the death penalty was restored, and there were stormy scenes in the Senate. In Britain there was a new leader of the Liberal Party after scandal had removed the old, and Denis Neilsen (also a multiple-murderer, but differently spelled, and mainly of sub-postmasters), whom the press called 'The Black Panther', was tried and convicted of the murder of Lesley Whittle, the Shropshire heiress, before Mr Justice Mars-Jones, while the judge's son sat in court making notes for a novel. In the village the final preparations were being made for the Flower Show.

Then as now the village activists were in thrall to the

Flower Show; like the Parish Council, the Flower Show Committee met throughout the year. Every year since at least the early sixties the Flower Show has taken more money than the year before, and must therefore continue to do so for all the years there are until Armageddon, although the Committee members grow older and the newcomers to the village less and less interested. Every year the cost of what always looks like the same marquee increases, and the reserve held to meet that cost must be proportionately greater, so that it sometimes seems as if the profits of the Flower Show are no longer devoted to the Village Hall or Cancer Research, but to paying for the marquee for next year's Show. Every year there must be more sideshows than the year before and the Special Attraction must be even more special.

Sideshows? Special Attraction? Did you believe that the Flower Show was devoted only to the showing of flowers, or at least produce? There may have been a time when that was so, but by the summer of the septic tank that time had long since passed. The Flower Show certainly had its traditional elements. None of the classes or conditions of entry had been changed for many years, and the Madeira Cake, judged by Mrs Fletcher and Mrs Hargreaves, still had to be baked to a recipe laid down during the Second World War and containing powdered egg. But every year, in addition to the Tea Tent and the Beer Tent, the Clay Pigeon Shooting and the Pig Roast, there were more sideshows and more stalls, Six-a-Side Football for teams drawn from most of the neighbouring villages or the Flower Show Committee's own version of *Jeux Sans Frontières*, a Dog Show and a Special Attraction which might be a Parade of Vintage Cars, formation riding by motorcyclists who also leapt through rings of fire, Show Jumping, the Massed Band and Glee Club of the local Comprehensive School (not a success, I fear), and, as it was this year, a Fly Past and Parachute Descent by the Yankee Daredevils from the USAF base at Upper Heyford.

The girls came down to the Flower Show in the after-

113

noon with Butch in a push-chair. They had entered tomatoes and French beans, their usual platter of exotic vegetables and their usual bottle of elderflower wine, which was to be judged that year by Mr Charles Wood, the celebrated dramatist. Celebrated or no, he had better award the girls their usual First or there would be talk in the village.

They made a slow circuit of the inside of the marquee, holding Butch up to admire the choicer exhibits. Yes, their tomatoes had done well, and the French beans also in spite of a strong field of entries. The platter of exotic vegetables had very little competition, and yes, Mr Charles Wood had done the right thing by their dry elderflower and written a flattering commendation on the back of the red card. Mrs Marshall's arrangement of dried flowers and grasses had been placed second to that of a newcomer, a woman who was not even chapel, but in general the right people had received the right awards; there was nothing revolutionary. The girls passed by cakes and tartlets and came to the Children's Section, reserved for pupils of the village school. Elsie Heavitree, eleven, had won a Special Award for the Spirit of Peace, constructed entirely from used matches and the tops of milk bottles. Butch, under direction, clapped his hands together at the Spirit of Peace, and was cooed at by two total strangers. Then on to dahlias which, by general accord, were as good as they had ever been, though the sweet peas were neither one thing nor the other, and the gladioli had been badly affected by the drought. The girls gave and received congratulations as they made their progress.

They emerged from the marquee with Butch a little fretful from the heat. Six-a-Side Football was in progress, had been since two o'clock and would be until seven; teenagers in shorts and striped shirts made complicated patterns in the centre of the pitch or waited morosely for their turn behind the goalposts. Away on the far side of the field there was an exhibition of Scarecrows by the Young Farmers; the other two sides of the field were lined

114

with stalls and sideshows. It was too early for the Tea Tent, in which the girls could see Mrs Marshall, grim-faced at failure, mutilating a rock-cake. All around them were the sounds of the Show, the crack of gunfire from the Clay Pigeons, yelping from the Dog Show, the thud of the football in play and cries of plaintive encourage-ment from the teams' supporters, the sizzling of the pig on the spit, the clatter of empty beer cans hitting a litter-basket, a string of incomprehensible admonitions and announcements from the Public Address System which seemed to be having trouble with its false teeth, and the contented buzz of a crowd of people spending money. Which way should the girls go first? Although they had already contributed to the Flower Show as patrons, and had their names in the programme to prove it, they would be expected to shell out at the sideshows as well.

They guessed the weight of a cake, the name of a doll, and the number of beans in a jar. If they had guessed correctly they would know at the end of the Show. Most of the other sideshows required the exercise of some form of dexterity – the Coconut Shy, Bobbing for Apples, Skit-tles, Darts, a modified form of Hoop-La in which a brass curtain ring attached by string to a stick had to be cast over the neck of a bottle, and Racing Mice (in which the dexterity was supplied by the mice). The girls discovered, not for the first time, that they lacked dexterity. They won no coconuts. Even their mouse ran last. It did not matter. They took it in turns to hold an ice-lolly for Butch to lick, and entered into communion with the crowd.

Next the stalls. The sideshows were organised directly by the Flower Show Committee. The recruitment of volunteers to staff them and the provision of prizes would occupy a special sub-committee for months. The stalls required no such degree of organisation. Each consisted of a board resting on four bales of straw. They were rented for the day by stall-holders, who stocked them and kept the profit. Stall-holders were given to sneezing, but the rents were low. Bales of straw were much used at the Flower Show, both as tables and as protective walling.

The vicar, who was a martyr to hay fever, remembered particularly when the motorcyclists in their leathers had ridden the Wall of Death, and bales of straw had been strewn all over the football field as well as around it. They had tidied the bales away before leaping through fire, but that had been too late for the vicar, who had been carried, gasping, from the Show and left in the church to recover.

The girls would visit the stalls out of interest. They would not be required to spend money there since that would only be enriching the stall-holders. They knew what they would find. There would be home-made cakes and fudge, in which they would take a critical interest. There would be some crafts, mainly salad-servers, with perhaps a little hand-weaving, and perhaps fire-dogs of brass or wrought iron. There would be a great deal of tat, purchased in job lots at auction to be sold off to townies in holiday mood. There would be second-hand clothes, and copies of the *National Geographic* magazine and *The Readers' Digest Book of Birds*, and piles of pink and white coconut ice. They would look at the stalls, and then at the scarecrows, and by then Butch would be over-tired, and they would all go home.

Around them people were gazing upwards, and there was the sound of approaching aircraft, first heard among the other sounds and then alone as the other sounds died away. It would be the Special Attraction. The Public Address System crackled angrily, and stewards ran to clear the football players from the field; since the match in progress had not yet reached even half-time, the players were reluctant to leave. Then flying down the valley, dangerously low as it seemed to the people at the Show, there came a V of seven aircraft. They circled the field twice, and thereafter, still keeping strict formation, began to spiral higher and higher. Back went the heads of the spectators; necks could be heard cracking all over the ground. The V of aircraft flew higher and higher, until from the leading aircraft a single parcel dropped, and then more parcels, and more from all the seven, which reached the summit of their spiral and then headed back to base, while the parcels became mushrooms, each with its dependent crash-helmeted figure, floating serenely downwards. From the crowd there came a communal noise, something between a sigh and a gasp, cut by the wail of a child who had realised that something momentous was happening and feared that it might do her harm, and then above that sound another, sharper, piping and jaunty, the sound of music. Reassured by the music, the child fell silent, and as the first of the Yankee Daredevils landed on top of the Tea Tent, Susan looked across the football field, and saw at the very furthest of the stalls a fat man with a beard playing a *bourrée* by George Frederick Handel on the ocarina.

9

THE VILLAGE POLICEMAN

Susan said, 'You take Butch back in the van. I'll walk up across the fields later. It's that friend of Alan's. He's got a stall. It can't be an accident.'

'Why can't we both go? He hasn't seen us.'

'He'd come to the house. I told you; it can't be an accident. Why should someone from Yorkshire take a stall selling early musical instruments at our Flower Show? He's come looking.'

'He'll probably come to the house anyway. We can't very well hide Butch in a cupboard.' Once peaceful villagers used to conceal their infants from marauders under the bed-linen in wooden presses or among the hay in the barn, but it did no good; the Vikings or marauding Highlanders always plunged swords into the bed-linen and set fire to the hay. 'We'll just have to brave it out. If he knew anything for certain, he'd have been before.'

'We'll brave it out together if we have to. Meanwhile I'd better have a go at braving it out on my own.'

The Special Attraction had been applauded by the crowd, and photographed for the local press, and the Public Address system had expressed what most listeners took to be thanks. More of the Yankee Daredevils had come to ground around the football field than on it, but only the one who landed astride the roasting pig had suffered any damage, and his burns, although embarrassing in their location, were superficial. He waited between Car Park and Dog Show for the arrival of an

118

ambulance, his lower half covered with a blanket, sustained by warm beer and the sympathy of those owners whose dogs had already been eliminated. There was general agreement that the Special Attraction had been a success, and would provide food for conversation during weeks to come. Meanwhile the Six-a-Side Football was resumed, and the crowd milled contentedly among the canvas walling and the bales of straw, from marquee to the two Refreshment Tents, from tombola to jumble, up and down the lines of stalls and sideshows. The next event of any consequence would be the presentation of the prizes, but few people stayed for that.

Susan walked slowly, stopping here to ask a price, there to praise a well-turned salad-server, lingering by the drop-earrings and the anodised copper pendants. It would not do for her approach to appear purposeful; she must seem to happen across the man. It might be helpful if she could remember his name. 'Hullo!' she would say, with the accent on the second syllable, 'It's . . .? You're . . .?' But as she drew nearer he began to play again, so that there was a small crowd surrounding him by the time she arrived at the stall, and she found herself in the second row, watching, all the dialogue she had prepared for an accidental encounter clearly wasted.

He finished the cheerful little tune, sold a couple of ocarinas for three pounds each, grinned at her and waved as if they had met only the day before, and beganshowing an eleven-year-old how to play the instrument, while the rest of the crowd dissipated leaving Susan standing there like a groupie. 'Shan't be a moment,' he said, and then to the child, 'Put your fingers here, and blow.' There seemed to be only ocarinas on the stall, some brightly coloured and some plain terracotta.

'Have you sold many?'

'Some.'

Susan decided to move onto the attack. 'It seems a long way to come to sell ocarinas. Are you sure you'll make a profit?'

'I thought I might combine it.'

119

'With what?'

'Visiting you?'

'Oh! . . . Well, it's very kind of you, of course, but are you sure we know each other well enough? And it's usual to phone first.'

'I have been before.'

'Yes.'

'You gave us tea and showed us round the garden. I remembered that.'

Susan felt like observing that her previous hospitality had obviously been a mistake if it had only encouraged him to drop in whenever he felt like it, but did not. She must tread warily. Being rude to the man might discourage him from coming up to the house, but might also provoke him into wondering why she was anxious to keep him away.

'I wanted to ask you about Alan.'

'Alan?'

'If you'd seen him at all.'

'Alan?'

'My partner. He was with me when we visited your house. Put it more exactly, I was with him. He'd teamed up with your friend Jan at Sykehouse, and hoped to see her again. I'm surprised you've forgotten him.'

'Oh, Alan! Of course I remember. How rude of me!' (*Don't overdo it, Susan.*) 'He's been on our conscience. We had a Christmas card from him, but I'm afraid we don't send them ourselves.' (*Lies! Lies! Beware unnecessary lies!*) 'We haven't seen him since. I hope he wasn't offended.'

'More hurt, I should think. He spent a lot of time choosing it.'

'I'm very sorry.'

'But you haven't seen him?'

'We haven't been to any Craft Fairs for over a year, except a few local ones. We decided it wasn't cost-effective.'

'Alan didn't have many friends, you see. He didn't have any really, only me. He thought he might have made

120

a friend of your Jan. That's why he was rather reluctant to lose her.'

How much did he know about Alan and Jan? How much did men talk to each other about these things? He was a fat man with a beard. Susan associated such men with lubricious laughter in saloon bars. But he was also a serious musician, specialising in – well, the classics: baroque or romantic, it was all classical music to Susan, who had learned to like the bits Jan liked, and did not otherwise differentiate. She did not think Alan would have boasted about making a sexual conquest, but if they were close friends – oh shit! The man was waiting for her to say something.

'Yes, I can understand that. Jan said he was very nice.' (*Careful! Are you talking about him in the past tense?*) 'She was sorry to miss him when you came to tea.' This was much more difficult than Susan had thought. First, the use of the past tense. She must remember that not only had neither she nor Jan seen Alan for nearly a year but, as far as they both knew, he was alive and in Yorkshire; they did not even know that he had left home. Why had she not begun by asking this man why Alan was not with him? 'Alan? Alan? Oh, Alan!' – what idiocy, from which she must now recover. 'I'm surprised you've not brought him with you. I hope he's all right.'

'You haven't seemed very surprised until now.'

'Well, you were busy with the little boy.' She looked about her. Why couldn't some other music-loving small child or even adult come to the stall and divert him from this line? 'I should have thought that if he wants to keep in touch, he'd have jumped at the chance of coming down.'

'He's disappeared.'

'Oh!'

'Took off one morning in March when I was away. Told his mother that he was going to London for a few days. I thought he might have looked in here.'

'Why should he?'

'Oh, come on; we've been into that. I don't know why you're fencing.'

121

He could not know, nobody could know, that she had killed Alan with a butter pat. It was so unlikely that nobody would suspect it. It came to Susan that if she had begun by telling the man that Alan had called, stayed the night, and gone on to London, he would have gone away satisfied. 'Better have a go at braving him on my own' – she had made a botch of it. Yet surely, as long as Alan's bones remained in the septic tank, they must deny that he had ever visited? That was the plan. It had not anticipated enquiries by the man with the beard, but it was the plan, and they must stick to it. There was something called carbon-dating by which even bones could be identified, some bones, so far mainly of prehistoric people preserved in peat bogs. Susan's knowledge of modern scientific developments was derived from skimming the Sunday papers, so there were gaps in it, but she had heard of the peat-bog people, and wasn't there something about a mummified Pharaoh who had been discovered to have suffered from osteoarthritis?

Better attack again. 'Well, I'm sorry you think I'm fencing, but you seem to be accusing me of something I know nothing about. If your friend's left home, it's nothing to do with Jan and me.'

'I just thought you might have seen him.'

'And you've come all the way to the village Flower Show just to find that out? What difference would it make if we had seen him? You didn't believe he could still be here?'

'It hasn't been all loss, you know. I have sold some ocarinas.'

There was beginning to be an audience again, but of a different kind from that attracted by his playing. Mrs Gaines had found some item of absorbing interest on the second-hand clothing stall, and was examining it with her head cocked on one side so as to keep her good ear within range of their conversation, while on the other side of the stall two women and a man, all three unknown to Susan, lingered in contemplation of the scarecrows. That she did not know them did not mean that they were not of the village; there were more village people who would recognise Susan than Susan would recognise.

Bob said, 'Look! We've got off on the wrong foot. I'll pack the stall up, and we can talk, Would you like some tea? We could go to the tent.'

'I have to go back for tea. Anyway I don't see that there's anything to talk about.'

She had made him cross. His face had gone sulky, and his lips twitched between beard and moustache. It is always a mistake to anger people, as Jan had so often told her when she, herself enraged at some injustice or imagined slight, some piece of shoddy workmanship or sharp commercial practice, had wished to rush into battle, all cannons blazing. (*'What good can it do?' 'It makes me feel better.' 'That's not enough.'*) Now the man, provoked, would say something disastrous. Already Mrs Gaines had edged a little nearer, holding the blouse she was examining up to the light, and the eleven-year-old who had bought the ocarina had returned, and was listening without concealment. Sue could not bear men with beards.

Could she bring herself to apologise? *'I'm sorry. I've been terribly rude. Of course you're worried about your friend. I wish I could help you'* – that would do it. It would give Mrs Gaines something to chew on, because the village did not know who Butch's father had been, and this conversation with a strange man, reported from house to house, would encourage speculation. But it would do no damage; speculation there already was, and would continue to be for all the years of Butch's growing-up. She must placate the man. She could not invite him back to the house for tea because of Butch, but it would do no harm to go with him to the Tea Tent. She would be seen there with him, and would have to explain him to Mrs Marshall later, but that was not a worry since Mrs Marshall already knew all there was to know. And Mrs Marshall would take care of the village speculation.

While Sue worked through this process of thought, she stared at the man, and even as she forced herself to the commonsense conclusion, her hatred of his beard (and his fatness; she also hated fat men) grew. Her face became pinker, her brow more moist, and just as she had reached the point when she felt able to turn decision into action and speak the placatory words, the hateful fellow said, 'I scent a mystery,' and it was already too late.

'No, you don't.'

Mrs Gaines said, 'Is this man bothering you, Susan?'

'No, he isn't. It's just someone I met up north, asking about a mutual friend,' and then to Bob, 'I'm so sorry. I really would like to have helped. I must go now,' and she was away, striding across the football field, almost bumping into the players in her anxiety to get away, the back of her neck a dusky red with every freckle clearly defined.

Mrs Gaines looked after her, and so did Bob, and the eleven-year-old and the three people who had given up pretending to look at the scarecrows. Susan's walk was the walk of someone who knows she is being watched. Bob said, 'I didn't mean to upset her.'

He picked up an ocarina from the stall, one of the coloured ones, a dark blue, and began to play, but this time a mournful tune. *'Che faro senza Eurydice? . . . Che faro, dove andro?'* It is what Orpheus sings in Gluck's opera, when he has turned to find his wife at his feet once more dead. Again he had chosen a moment when the crowd was more silent than not: the Public Address System was having its tea, the dogs had all been judged, and the clay pigeons all shattered. Susan could hear the little tune clearly as she reached the other side of the field, but it meant no more to her than its being one of those pieces of music Jan liked, and not particularly well suited to the ocarina.

Mrs Marshall walked up across the fields next morning after chapel. 'Now what was that all about?' she said.

'Aren't you having Sunday dinner with Ralph?'

124

'You can drive me down in a bit. I wouldn't say no to a glass of that sherry. I'm all of a muck sweat.'

For a short period of her life, not long after she had left the care of the auntie who had reared her, Mrs Marshall had been in service in a good house. She had never taken kindly to being ordered about, nor had her employers been altogether comfortable in the presence of a house-maid of six foot two. She had left in 1933 by mutual agreement a week after her twenty-first birthday, which she had celebrated by blacking the eye of a baronet. One of the scraps of knowledge she had picked up during this period of her life was that the gentry preferred their sherry dry, and she had trained herself to acquire the taste for it.

The sherry was called Fino Elegante, and was kept specially for Mrs Marshall. The girls themselves drank wine of their own making, and offered it to their rare guests. However, to ask for a glass of sherry in the middle of the day, even on a Sunday, was unusual and must be construed as a signal that Mrs Marshall had done the girls some service which she wished to celebrate. Jan said, 'A friend of Butch's father came asking questions.'

'Can't have that.'

'No, that was what we thought.'

'Only cause talk. Cheers!'

Sherry was sipped. Mrs Marshall savoured it. Susan said, 'I made rather a mess of things, though.'

'As I heard.' The girls looked at each other. 'Stamped off in a paddy, and left him playing music at your back.'

Janet said, 'Was there any talk about what he was playing?'

'Something classical.'

Susan had la-laed the tune to Janet on her return, and it had been identified. 'It's sung by someone whose wife has just died. It's a lament. What's he going to do without her? – that sort of thing.'

'Cheeky object! Beryl Gaines told me he'd been making himself objectionable. Hinting. She didn't hear it all.'

'How much did she hear?'

125

'Thought his friend might have been to see you. Something about a Christmas card. Told Sue she was fencing.'

'Most of it, then?'

'Couldn't make anything of it, though. Thought he was trying to pick Sue up. Angling. Then he plays his pipe. Stupid! Thought he was a bloody snake-charmer, by all accounts. Standing there with a great belly on him, playing his pipe, and Sue walking through the football, red as fire. All Beryl could do not to laugh, but she could see Sue was upset, so she held it in, and came to find me at the jumble.'

'And what did you do?'

'Sent him away with a flea in his ear. "You pack up and go," I said, "or I'll speak to the Committee." Stood over him while he loaded his car. Silly little blobby things, like goose-eggs with holes cut in! "I don't call *that* a pipe," I said, "I could have you up before the Trades Descriptions Act. We don't want your sort here, so you can bugger off, and be quick about it." And he did. Bloody object! You won't hear much of him again.'

Bob had driven away along the Stratford road, angry and perplexed. He did not know who the woman was who had hustled him. She had seemed to represent outraged village opinion, but he did not know how he had outraged it. There had been another woman hovering a little way behind her for much of the time, the woman who had been pretending to examine a blouse at the second-hand clothing stall, and who had asked Susan if he had been bothering her. Were all the women of the village in league? Even if they were, Susan and this Jan whom he had never met were clearly not of the village, living on the hill outside, coming from outside, of a different class. Why should the village women protect them? The tall woman was clearly a power in the village. 'I'll speak to the Committee' – and if she had, he had no doubt they would have paid attention. All he had done was to ask

126

Susan whether she or her friend had seen Alan. One would think they would want to help.

There was something odd about it, the whole business. That girl knew something. When he and Alan had come before, she had got rid of them just as soon as she decently could. They had only had her word that her friend was in Evesham. *"She's not very friendly, your friend."* *"It's her friend that's friendly."*

He had come on the off-chance, no more than that, bringing ocarinas to defray the expense of the expedition. He had come because he had had to do something, and the police would do nothing. They had entered Alan on the police computer as a missing person, and that was it. Bob had gone to the station himself; he had spoken to the desk sergeant. He had explained that Alan was extremely responsible, almost neurotically so, punctilious about never letting people down. If anything had delayed his return from London, he would have telephoned, he would have written, he would have returned as soon as he could. But there was no evidence, the desk sergeant had said, that a crime had been committed; to disappear was not a crime. Bob had argued that Alan's whole temperament and personality were evidence. Not in a court of law. The sergeant was being as helpful as he could, and would be even more helpful if allowed the opportunity, but he had to have evidence before he could set into operation the elaborate machinery of a search by and on behalf of the West Yorkshire Constabulary. What kind of evidence? Bloodstained clothing, said the sergeant. But they had no clothing at all, bloodstained or otherwise; Alan had been wearing it. A large amount of money drawn from a joint account. Alan had his own bank account, which had never amounted to more than three figures.

Something stolen from the shop. Bob had been tempted to lie, but the vision of Alan hitch-hiking to London with a purloined shawm or rebeck stuffed inside his jacket would not hold up. In that case, the desk sergeant had said, the most advisable course of action would be to wait, because the missing person usually turned up. When that happened, perhaps Bob or the young man's parents would be kind enough to let him know so that they could remove the young man from the computer.

It was so unfair. It was so wrong. The desk sergeant had agreed that the system was not without its difficulties, but the law was the law, and the police were always under pressure.

One could wait for so long, and then one had to act. Bob did not particularly like Alan's parents, but they seemed to grow smaller from week to week, and he could not bear that. There were only ten years between himself and Alan, but he himself had been in some ways more like a father to the boy, particularly after he and Rachel had split, silly cow. Alan's real father had not acted, but waited as he had been told to do; Bob had decided to act. This Janet had been only a small lead to investigate, but it was obvious that something had happened at Syke house, obvious that Alan had wanted to impress her and her friend, obvious that he had tried to keep the contact and create a relationship of some sort. It was so unlikely that Alan would just take off for London, where he knew nobody, but he might have planned a trip to London if he could have used the occasion to make a diversion.

She knew something. *"Alan? . . . Alan? . . . Oh, Alan!"* It had been unconvincing. She had been trying to put him off, but from what?

He had considered turning the car, driving back to the girls' home, and having it out with them, but had not known what he would say, and if there were a complaint made, backed up by the Flower Show women, that first he had harassed the younger girl, and then forced himself on the two of them in their own home, it might make trouble for him. It would not be a police matter, but there might be publicity, and the girls were in the craft business and if they were to complain that he had abused his position as a stall-holder, he might be barred from Fairs far more important than a village Flower Show. Anyway

128

he had needed time to think; he could return later if he decided to do so.

He imagined himself returning to the desk sergeant. 'I've got this new evidence.' 'Yes?' 'I went down to a village Flower Show, and interviewed a young woman who'd met Alan in the past. I asked if she'd seen him lately, and she became evasive.' 'And the evidence, sir?' 'That's it. She became evasive.' Oh, shit!

It was no good. Bob was not a policeman. He had no authority to interrogate the girls, and no experience of conducting an interrogation. Yet the police would not do it, not the West Yorkshire Constabulary; they would not even ask the local police to do it for them. Driving away from the Flower Show towards Stratford, Bob had entertained bitter thoughts about the police. Missing persons, battered wives, it was all the same; the police did not regard the alleviation of human distress as being their concern.

He had not been driving fast. To drive fast when one is in a bad temper is asking for trouble. He had passed the entrance to what looked like a lane, unmetalled and overgrown, leading off the road, and had glimpsed a vehicle parked a little way in. It was blue and white. Did he imagine that it was a police vehicle because his own bitter thoughts had been concerned with the police? On impulse he pulled in to the side of the road a little way past the lane.

He sat in the car trying to decide why he had stopped. What if it were a police car, what was that to do with him? But if he could talk, just talk over his suspicions, not with the unhelpful desk sergeant but with some local policeman who would know the girls, even if it did no more than calm him, that would be something. Well, it would do no harm to go and look. The vehicle might be an abandoned ice-cream van, in which case he would have wasted a few minutes, and that would be it, but if he did not look, he would spend the whole journey wondering whether he had spotted a police car in the lane or not; he would wake up in the middle of the night

129

convinced that he had, and be unable to go back to sleep. He left his own car, and walked a little way back towards the entrance to the lane, stopped and dithered. What would he say? 'I saw your car in the lane, and stopped for a bit of a word.' The police might be lying in wait for some major criminal, and would not be pleased; the interruption might bring weeks of planning to nothing. Well, he would look into the lane, and if the car were full of policemen wearing tense expressions, he would go away again quickly, and if they took him for one of the gang, well that would be inconvenient, but he could explain.

It was not a car; it was a van, but a police van sure enough. It was parked a little way up the lane, and could not be lying in wait for criminals because it was pulled a little way into the side and facing away from the road. Bob wondered why that should be. Cattle-rustlers? But not in broad daylight on a Saturday afternoon in summer. He found himself walking up the lane towards the van, with his anger beginning to return. Bloody policemen! It was typical of them to be idling in country lanes when they could be out searching for missing persons.

There was no room to approach the van on the driver's side. He looked through the window of the passenger side, and saw a young police constable with butter-coloured hair who appeared to be biting the neck of a teenage girl. The girl's own hair looked as if it belonged in a television commercial; it was long and blonde and silky, giving evidence of a healthy diet and expensive shampoo. The constable's left arm was round the girl's shoulders with his hand among the hair at the back of her head, touching and caressing, enjoying its softness against the hard bone of her neck and skull, while his right hand was engaged in squeezing and manipulating her left breast beneath her shirt, which had been unbuttoned for this purpose. The girl's own right hand was at work in the constable's lap, and he had his mouth at her throat, and was expressing his enjoyment of all this

130

complicated cocktail of sensations by making little moans of pleasure.

Bob knocked on the window of the van. The constable's head jerked sharply upwards, striking the girl under the chin. At the same time, the two of them tried to pull apart. Both these operations seemed to cause the girl pain, and she grabbed the constable's left arm and tried to hold it where it was.

'Don't!'

Bob opened the door of the van on the passenger side. 'Can I help at all?'

'He's got his watch-strap caught in my hair.'

It was one of those cheap watch-straps made of metal links, and the girl's hair had become tangled with several of them. It would not be easy to untangle without causing further pain. Bob said, 'Would both of you please keep absolutely still?' It was lucky that he was used to delicate work with hair and gut. As Bob carefully separated strands of exquisitely groomed upper-class hair from metal, he saw in the eyes of the police constable gazing up at him the expression of a pure hatred, and it occurred to him that the interview had not begun on the right foot. It occurred to him also that the two of them would have had this problem anyway, whether he had knocked on the window of the van or not, but he decided not to mention it.

Bob had blundered into what was to become a major scandal in the village before the year was out. The girl was Fiona, youngest of the children of the Manor, and the only daughter. The police constable was Duncan, who, as has been remarked, was well accustomed to entertaining local girls and mature ladies also in his van, usually in the back where he kept a foam-rubber mattress and a glass ash-tray. Local policemen are not often local, since it is embarrassing to have to arrest a childhood friend; Duncan had come south from Morecambe, and in eighteen months made his presence felt; his whole life stretched before him, a butter-coloured pathway of pleasure and promotion. Then he met Fiona, a girl out of his class, and became besotted. As for Fiona, she had been strictly reared in the country and schooled by Anglican nuns, and Duncan's steady application and constant readiness to please provided an experience altogether outside her range. He had always been cautious, but now ceased to be. She had never found caution attractive; if she was to have an affair, she would flaunt it. Her parents behaved hysterically. Treated with patience and respect, Duncan would easily have been induced to "wait" for Fiona, which would have allowed her time to tire of him. Instead he received bluster and threats, and she persuaded him to run away with her. They did not run far, only to Solihill. He was dismissed from the police force, and with difficulty obtained a job as a travelling salesman for a firm making security devices. Most of their income came from his commission, which fluctuated from week to week and mainly downwards; also he was often away from home. Within a year, Fiona returned to her parents. He followed her. She refused to see him. He neglected his travelling and hung about the village, trying to engage old acquaintances in conversation. He began to drink, lost the job, and then his licence to drive; in any case he could not keep up the payments on the car. By that time, unemployment was already widespread in the West Midlands, and no one wanted an ex-policeman who drank. He lived where he could, mainly on social security, but never far from the village. Fiona's father obtained a court order to prevent his hanging about outside the Manor. Fiona herself was studying fashion design in Milan, but it proved impossible to make Duncan understand that she was no longer in the country; he could not take it in. He had been so trim and butter-coloured and apt for love, and now he was a mess. Mrs Lacey, a divorcée who had known him in the old days and remembered the Dunlopillo mattress and the glass ash-tray, took him in hand for a while and tried to make something of him, but it did no good; he had lost all his application. Late one night in the winter of 1984, still not out of his twenties, he ended his life as an untidy parcel, stained

132

with blood and vomit, on the side of the A34, the victim of a hit-and-run driver.

But that is a different story of village life. In the summer of 1976, Duncan's aspirations were still high. This was the first time out with Fiona. The rest was yet to come.

Bob said, 'There! That'll do it. Move your arm gently. I'm glad I found you.'

'Bloody peeping Tom! I know your sort.'

'Oh no, nothing like that. I was driving past, and spotted your van in the lane. Extremely good luck!' Both Duncan and Fiona stared at him, speechless. 'For me, I mean. Perhaps I could have a word if it's not too much trouble.'

'There's a police station in Stratford. It's continually manned.'

'Aren't you the village policeman?' It occurred to Bob that, given the use to which the young constable was putting his van, he might be operating some way from base.

'There's no such thing these days.'

Bob could recognise evasion when he heard it. 'You mean you are?'

'We may be based on villages, but we work shifts, same as anyone else. And I'm off-duty at the moment, so you can bugger off and be quick about it.'

It was the second time Bob had been told to bugger off in one afternoon, and he found he did not care for it. 'If you're off-duty, would you kindly explain to me why you're in uniform and why you're making use of an official vehicle?'

'That'll do from you.'

'No,' said Bob. 'It won't. I'm sorry. It won't. I've made no comment so far on what you're doing in uniform – well, partly out of it; you can zip yourself up for a start – and in a police vehicle with a girl who looks under age to me, because it's not my business . . .'

'Right!'

'– but you and me will have a word together, confidentially in private, or I shall make it my business. There's a police station in Stratford, you say? And continually manned? I'll take the number of the van.'

There was a silence, and then Duncan opened the door on his side, and stepped out into long grass and campion.

Consequently the girls had a second visitor that Sunday. Duncan arrived at tea-time. They gave him tea in the conservatory, and by unspoken agreement Jan was left to deal with him, since she was the older and had experience of the police from her days in the probation service. This was made to seem all the more natural by the chance that Butch, whether excited by the uniform, aggrieved at competition or just fretful with the heat, made one of his rare decisions to play up, so that Susan was forced to entertain him elsewhere.

'Suspicious of what?' Janet said.

'He couldn't say. Just in a general way.'

'Well, I don't blame him for feeling frustrated. Can't the police where he lives help him?'

'Not without evidence of a crime. It's standard procedure. I told him.'

'But you're helping him?'

'On an unofficial basis.' Duncan bit into cake. 'He was very upset. I found him wandering in a lane.' Janet's gaze was not hostile, but it was what is called 'level', polite and direct with a hint of inquiry. It was the sort of gaze which might make a man wish that he had come better prepared. 'What he felt was, you see, he felt that Miss Burt was. . . .'

'Fencing. That was the accusation.'

'Hiding something. Had something to hide. I said I'd make enquiries on an unofficial basis.'

'You mean you don't intend to make an official report?'

'No. That is, not unless . . . I mean, I'd have to make a report if there was evidence of a crime having been committed, but not otherwise.'

'I see. More cake?' Duncan refused cake. 'Tea?' He

134

accepted another cup of tea with two sugars. 'Well, he's right. Susan was hiding something, but it certainly wasn't evidence of any crime.' Duncan had never believed it would be. 'I'm going to have to take you into our confidence, Duncan, but I'd be grateful if you didn't spread it round the village.'

'I'm not local. You know that.'

'Yes, I do. Well. . . .' Insofar as it is possible to do so when seated in a reclining chair, Duncan assumed an atittude of respectful attention. 'A couple of years ago, I met Alan, the young man who's disappeared, up north at a Craft Fair. We were both on our own, and we got rather friendly, and ended up in bed. You can understand that.' Duncan blushed. 'I wasn't on the pill, but he didn't know that. Butch was the result. I never told Alan. It wasn't anything to do with him.' If there had been any doubt in Duncan's mind that he was on Janet's side, it evaporated with that remark. 'He tried to keep in touch; apparently he hasn't many friends. He and this man Bob came visiting last year, but I was away, and they never saw Butch. Alan doesn't know that he's the father, and that's the way I want to keep it. When Susan saw Bob at the Flower Show yesterday, she thought the two of them were at it again, dropping in unannounced, and they'd discover about Butch. That was what she was hiding, and when she found out that what Bob really wanted was help because Alan had disappeared, it was too late, and anyway she couldn't explain. So she beat a retreat in some confusion, and left him suspicious.'

'That's it, then, isn't it?' Duncan said. 'She was hiding something, but it wasn't what he thought she was hiding.'

'What did he think she was hiding?'

'He didn't know. That's what made him suspicious.'

'However, no crime has been committed, so maybe we could keep it unofficial.'

'Oh, yes!'

'And you can understand that I'd rather it weren't spread about the village?'

'Don't you worry, Janet.' She had used his first name,

135

so he supposed he could use hers. He wondered whether she might be a good fuck, and decided that she probably would. He preferred teenagers as a rule because they would settle for action without endearments, whereas older ladies, unhappy in their marriages or already abandoned, were forever demanding emotional reassurance. He did not think that Janet would make such demands; she seemed to be a cool one; they could just get on with it, in the back of the van or wherever. 'I can keep my mouth shut. Don't you worry. The soul of discretion.' The problem with Janet, Duncan decided, would be how to make the first approach, and anyway her friend was always with her. Luckily it was not a problem of immediate concern, since Fiona had not been put off by Bob's interrupting them, quite the contrary, and they had a date for the evening. He was into a piece of real class there, no doubt of it. He decided to store up his speculation about Janet for later use, and meanwhile to cement the relationship. 'You can rely on me.'

He would respect her confidence, as he had promised, but there was still the matter of the bearded fatso. The arrangement was that Duncan was to write to Bob within a week, telling him the result of the unofficial enquiry, and when Bob received the letter he would forget what he had seen in the van. If he did not receive it, he would write a letter himself, but it would be to the Personnel Officer at Division. Suppose Duncan were to write that he had pursued enquiries, and was satisfied that no crime had been committed. That would be the truth, but it was unlikely to satisfy Bob, who would only believe that Duncan had gone back on the bargain. Yet if Duncan were to pass on what Janet had told him, he would not only be breaking a confidence, but laying up trouble for her when the missing young man turned up again and was informed by his friend that he had become a father.

Driving back slowly from the girls' house to the police cottage, Duncan pondered this dilemma, which had a moral dimension as so many dilemmas have. They had been strong on natural morality during his training as a police cadet, and encouraged it so long as it did not come into conflict with the law. Then there was Duncan's own good opinion of himself, which he had long cherished, and did not wish to lose. However, he had to get the letter into the post that evening and meet Fiona at nine-thirty outside the Manor, so he sat down as soon as he got in, and wrote to Bob.

10

INTERLUDE

Sue said, 'It's two years since I was in Crete. There's a lot happened since, I must say. You never wear that shirt I bought you.'

'It's too tight across the tits.'

'That's nonsense; they're back to normal and you know it. You and your bloody stretch marks!'

Sue's present to Jan, brought back from the package tour, had been an authenticated copy of an ikon, which she had bought at a small shop in the streets behind the harbour at Chania. She had not been sure what 'authenticated' meant as applied to copies of ikons, but it had seemed better than an ordinary copy, and she had spent much of the holiday looking for something special which would cost a lot, and had become desperate by the last day. Neither of the girls liked it very much, but it was kept on the dresser in the bedroom, and dusted regularly. She had also brought back a shirt of thick rough white cotton with a blue vertical stripe, made in the Greek style with no collar or buttons, just a slit at the neck. Jan had worn it constantly until her breasts swelled with milk, and thereafter not at all, though she had long since ceased suckling. She had expected, and therefore accepted, stretch marks on her belly, but was self-conscious about the corrugations round her nipples, and preferred a top which would button up to the neck.

Although, by early October, the summer still did not seem to be over, they had taken to closing the shop on

138

Mondays. They remained committed to it, of course, since they considered it to be their living, but there had been a steady growth in mail order, and Mondays were never particularly busy days for passing trade, and anyway a couple should be together whenever possible to enjoy their baby; the books said so. The girls sat together in reclining chairs in the conservatory this Monday after a late lunch, with Butch on the pot in Janet's lap. He had only recently been introduced to the pot, at first on the principle that it was up to him to make what he would of it, since any form of coercion, even of direction, was likely to be counter-productive. So far he had found two uses for it. One was to push it about the floor, the other to wear it as a helmet. The girls had decided to amend the principle. They would allow themselves to be directive to this extent, that they would sit him on it in comforting and comfortable circumstances and at a time when evacuation might be thought likely, and would reward him with the most fulsome praise if he were to use it for its intended purpose. They had been working on this amended principle for a week, and had not so far had occasion to reward Butch with praise.

'Two years!'

'And a month.'

'I hated it. And then so much after. All the worry and . . . the excitements and. . . .' Susan found that she did not wish to be specific after that "and". There had been wonderful times, but there had been other times. They were over now, since the Flower Show, and if she had not already begun to put them behind her she would not have been able to speak of them in such a relaxed way. It was odd how quickly one could forget. Well, not forget, not exactly forget, but to behave like someone at the beginning of a different time.

'This is no good. I'll take him off, and get him back into those bloody pants. Asking for trouble.' Butch began to complain. 'All right, Butchles, you can come back on my lap when your bottom's covered.' It was just over seven weeks, and Duncan had seemed satisfied, nor had he or any of his colleagues returned to question the girls further, but even so Jan thought it better not to tempt providence. 'You sound as if you're putting it all safely into the past tense.'

'Well, it is all in the past tense. Not the shirt; I want you to bring that back into the present. But everything else.'

'Past and present, they're all the same. And the future. All ifs. If you hadn't been sent to that dreadful school at King's Sutton, we'd never have met.'

'You and I would always have met somehow. That was meant.'

'The nightmares have gone, then?' Jan kept her face turned away, and concentrated on getting Butch smoothly into the all-in-one disposable nappy.

'Yes, I think so. Flies gone, smell gone, nightmares gone. And I'm sleeping; I'm not so tense; you must have noticed. It is the past. I wonder sometimes. I think about going into the shrubbery, and moving the slabs to see if he's still there, but that's when I'm awake, and it's curiosity, not fear. I mean, I'm not drawn to him, the way murderers are.'

'It wasn't murder.'

'Right. I suppose the bones must get separated after a bit.' Jan nodded. 'Alas, poor Yorick! I suppose the skeletons you see in museums are strung together.' Like most people, Susan had never seen a skeleton, in a museum or anywhere else, and her notion of what one looked like was put together from comic strips, cartoon films and the illustrations to medical encyclopaedias. 'I suppose they just separate and sink to the bottom. I suppose it'll happen to us.'

'Much worse than that, my girl, may happen to us. Why else did I make you give up smoking?'

'Anyway we're going to be cremated. No skeletons. They'll shovel us in together, and Butch can scatter our ashes over the potato patch. Be a good crop that year.'

'There! All done! Do you want the pot? Want to push

140

it around a bit? Or shall I just put you back in your pants, and we'll pretend we never tried?'

Sue said, 'Well, I can't sit here, nattering. I've got to sow the cauli, and then start cutting that bloody hedge.'

'You're always cutting it.'

'Twice a year. I can remember when you used to hold the steps.'

Was Susan jealous? She couldn't be. They shared everything to do with Butch, one of them with him always; that was the joy of it. But no, it had been a tease. Sue was wearing one of her wider grins, and every freckle glowed. This summer, because of the prolonged sunshine, there were more freckles than ever; they provoked lust. 'Oh God!' Janet thought, 'I'm ten years older; I shall die before her, but at least she'll still have Butch.' She did up the poppers on his trainer-pants, and held him up. 'Do you want to cuddle him for a bit?' But it was a false gesture; Butch was not a doll, and made angry noises at being treated as if he were.

'Too much to do.'

'Do you want to go to bed?' They could try putting him down for a nap, or simply leave him in his cot in the bedroom.

'Something's got into you. I don't know what.' Sue bent over, and kissed her. Sue's lips were warm, and she smelled of the sun; it was momentarily upsetting. 'I'm off.'

Butch had decided that he preferred Jan's lap, particularly now that it was potless, to a blanket on the floor, and scrambled to get back. She took him up, and reached out for the book they were reading. So far it had always been Jan who had done the actual reading, but sometimes Butch would point to a picture, and make sounds which might, by those with faith, be construed as an approximation to the name of what the picture represented, so that a generalised "ow" might be taken as "cow" or "house" or even "horse" or certainly "owl" and on one occasion "crocodile". Every day there was growth of some

141

kind, yet every day he was the more comfortingly the same.

Their book that afternoon had arrived recently from Janet's mother, and was to be read for the first time; most of their books were read often, since Butch preferred pictures he had seen before and actions accompanying them which were already familiar. It seemed about right to Janet, having pages of thick card, easily turned by small fingers but not easily torn, and was bountifully illustrated in four colours, with very little text. Perhaps the subject was a little too improving, a little too much her mother's taste, a little moralising in tone. It concerned Jill and Joe, who played in the garden, and refused to wash when they came indoors, so that the seeds germinated where they had lodged. Butch turned a page. *"Poor Jim! Look at him!"* Flowers grew from every finger, and his head was a hedge. Jan's eyes filled with tears. She raised her head to look across at the shrubbery, but the shrubs hid the septic tank, and in any case her vision was obscured. She wept silently, and Butch reached up at first out of curiosity to touch the tears, and then, discovering that he was no longer the entire object of Jan's attention, began angrily to strike at the side of her face.

Susan had gone out with line and draw-hoe to sow the cauliflowers. Last year she had brought them on in boxes, and sown them as young plants in March, but the curds had come too early and been caught by frost and snow. This year they would sit out the winter in the vegetable patch under cloches. A little peat had been dug into the ground, which had been well raked. She was using the area where the French beans had grown; the books said that the roots of leguminous vegetables fixed nitrogen in the soil. Susan was not sure how this process operated, and imagined little bubbles of nitrogen attached to the roots of the beans like witch-balls held by netting, but she did not have to know; she only had to follow the book. Susan did everything by the book. She liked to have authority for even the most insignificant acts. Her parents and the school at Winchelsea had much to answer for.

142

The line was a string attached to two bamboo canes. She stuck one of the canes into the prepared ground, and began to unwind the string; her line must be absolutely straight, as straight as every other line of vegetables in the patch. The time was going on two-forty-five, and the sun, always in the south at this season, had declined to the west, and was shining towards the woods. There was a flash of light, she noticed, and then again, almost like a heliograph, the rays of the sun reflected for a moment on turning glass at the edge of the woods. She stood up to look in that direction, but the flashing light had gone and was not repeated. It would be nothing important. There were the cauliflowers to sow, and then the hedge.

11

BULLOCKS

At Christmas the girls had a card from Alan. There was a London postmark, SW17. This time there was no return address inside the card, just greetings in four languages, as is usual with UNICEF cards, and Alan's name handwritten.

They would have compared the handwriting, but of course they had not kept his card of the year before; Mrs Marshall took all the Christmas cards every year for the schoolchildren to paste on screens which were sold, usually to the children's parents, in aid of Guide Dogs for the Blind. Did they know another Alan? No. The girls were surprised to discover, when one made a total, how few people they knew, and none in SW17. And in any case it was the same card, a design by Miro. They looked out a yellowing *A to Z of London*, and consulted that. SW17 was Streatham. Even if Alan were alive, what would he be doing in Streatham?

Perhaps he had written two cards the Christmas before, and kept one to send this year. Someone from Streatham would have discovered and posted it. The explanation was ludicrous, but hardly more so than that the girls had suffered a joint hallucination and imagined the whole episode, or put someone else in the septic tank while Alan went cheerily on to London in the rain.

The Christmas card perturbed the girls greatly, and in consequence they made a mistake. They did not write to Bob to tell him that they had received it. It is not an excuse that they did not know where Bob lived or even his second name. The names and addresses of dealers in early musical instruments are easily discovered; there are not so many. They might have phoned the Warwick Arts Centre, where Bob and Alan had both set up their stand in the October of 1975, or simply asked Duncan, who was still to be found in the police cottage, his downfall not yet begun.

Bob himself had recently been following a different line of enquiry, showing Alan's photograph at places of resort in Chelsea and Earl's Court, Notting Hill Gate and Hampstead, Paddington, Soho and King's Cross, but with no results of any consequence. He would have been interested and pleased to hear the girls' news; it would at least have allowed him to concentrate his search in a particular direction. Bob could not afford to diffuse his energies too widely; he had a living to earn. He had not so far replaced Alan with any other partner.

Time passed. Perturbation ebbed away. It was a mystery, and a worrying one, but seemed to have led nowhere. The girls kept it to themselves, did not even mention it to Mrs Marshall, and after a while there was nothing to keep but the memory of something odd; even the card itself had been taken off with the others and pasted on a screen. Then in March, on the very same day as that on which Alan had arrived the year before, a similar day of strong winds and the promise of rain, there was a postcard of Magdalen Bridge with the college in the background, sent from Oxford by first-class post the day before, and this time with a message, 'Hope to see you soon. Alan.'

Susan had collected the postcard from the box with the newspaper and the rest of the mail on her way from the shop for lunch. She threw the newspaper on the passenger-seat of the van, and looked, as she always did, at the letters. There was something from *The Readers' Digest* marked 'IMPORTANT. FOR YOUR IMMEDIATE ATTENTION'; it would be about winning £40,000 or an income for life in return for buying their condensed books.

There was a letter from the Diners' Club, addressed to 'Mr J. Hallas' (always infuriating, that), which would be inviting Janet, as a person of distinction in her field, to take advantage of a Special Introductory Membership. A typewritten envelope from Luton, also for Janet, second-class, therefore not important, and a letter for Susan herself, first-class and hand-written on a pale lavender envelope, which would be from her mother, complaining that Susan never wrote. And this postcard of some college in Oxford. She turned it over, and read what was written on the back.

The box was at the top of the track which led to the girls' house. There was half a mile to be driven slowly in thought. Susan's first impulse was to hide the card, but Jan would know that something was wrong, since Jan always knew. What could it mean? It was the Christmas card all over again, but worse. *"Hope to see you soon."* She parked the car, but did not go in immediately for lunch. Instead she went to the top of the rockery, and stood there, staring across at the shrubbery. There was no sun on this day to be reflected from the glass of binoculars, but there was a presence in the woods nevertheless, watching her.

Sue went indoors, and Jan knew at once, as Sue had known she would, that there was something wrong. Sue gave her the postcard. Jan read it, and said, 'Someone's playing silly buggers.'

'Who?'

'It's that bloody Duncan, isn't it? He's told somebody. "The soul of discretion"? I should have known. Mrs Marshall says he's having it off with that girl at the Manor.'

'But you had to explain.'

'Oh, yes. There wasn't any choice about that. He promised he'd keep his mouth shut. I suppose it's all over the village. Doesn't matter anyway. After all, Butch has to have a father somewhere. It wasn't spontaneous combustion.'

'If it was all over the village, Mrs Marshall would have told us.'

'Yes.' Jan was thoughtful. 'That means he's only told the girl at the Manor. Boasting to impress her.' She looked again at the postcard. 'She'd have friends in Oxford.'

'But why?'

'Mischief?'

A Christmas card from Streatham, a postcard from Oxford. The girl at the Manor would have friends in Streatham also, Sue supposed. She was still at boarding school, as Sue herself had been, where the girls came from all over; there had been twins from Bulawayo at the Winchelsea academy, said to have a touch of the tar brush, given to hysteria in the dorm when separated but demons on the hockey-field. "*Hope to see you soon.*" Why? All the Manor girl could know was all that Duncan knew, that Butch's father had been a one-night stand at the Inland Waterways Rally, and had since disappeared from his home in Yorkshire. "*Hope to see you soon.*" If it were mischief, what was its object? To put the girls into a panic that Alan was about to return and claim his son?

The girls at Winchelsea had frightened each other in the dorm with stories of the undead, misremembered from late-night television. Would the undead come back to claim a child? "*Having a son, it gives a meaning to your life, doesn't it?*" And she had hit him with the Scotch hand, and then pressed her body against his to bring him back to life, but failed. When Alan died he had only just discovered that he had a son at all. "*Hope to see you soon.*" Would he come back from the septic tank for Butch, pushing aside at dead of night the slabs which covered it, oozing through the shrubbery and across the lawn, reaching (green and naked and decaying) his arms into the cot?

After lunch, before returning to the shop, she put on wellies and a duffel, and went to look at the septic tank in the rain. The lawn was littered with twigs from the ash tree, blown down by March winds, and part of a dead branch had broken off and landed by the shrubbery.

147

Susan pulled the branch to the fence, and pitched it over into the field. That ash would have to go. Once part of the hedge but allowed by neglect to grow, it was now dying slowly, as is the way of trees. Thirty years ago the hedge had been reinforced by wire, one loop of it lashed around the main trunk of the ash, and as the ash had grown the wire had cut first into the bark then into the living wood of the trunk, every year deeper so that it could no longer be removed. The ash was garotting itself year by year with the rusty wire. It would be a kindness to fell it.

She stepped over daffodils in flower and pushed between berberis and dogwood to get at the tank. It looked as it looked, as it had always looked, the slabs green and lichenous, and the roots of nettles pushing into the brick. The slabs might have been moved and replaced; one could not tell; they did not fit exactly together. Susan herself had thought about moving the slabs out of mere curiosity; now she would move them out of a kind of necessity, almost out of bravado; she would defy her stars. *"Hope to see you soon"* But it was Susan who would see Alan soon, what was left of him. She pulled aside one slab and then another.

The rain shook in the wind like a curtain, hitting her face with its wet folds. What could she have expected to see in this weather? If she had looked beneath the slabs during last year's drought, then perhaps she might have seen something, the remnants of Alan sitting in filth against the side of a brick box. Perhaps that, perhaps not. As matters were, the septic tank was full to the brim with dark water and the faeces floating at the top. They had tipped him in a year ago. He had fallen face forwards, and his white bum had bobbed in the water to be pressed down with a concrete slab. She had half-expected to see the bones of that bum still in the same position, but Alan's pelvis would have fallen to the bottom of the tank with the other bones.

Janet watched from the conservatory, holding Butch up to look at the rain. He had seen a deal of rain already that

148

year, and did not reckon much to it, but he enjoyed being held if it were not for too long. *"Hope to see you soon."* She had told Sue that it was merely a piece of mischief, but she did not believe that herself, or anyway not yet. She had intended to reassure her friend, while giving herself the afternoon to think about what the message might mean. It occurred to her that perhaps that friend of Alan's, the hairy one, might have sent the card, but why? She could see Sue through rain and the bare bushes, heaving at a slab. So much for reassurance! What a strange girl Sue was, swinging from nightmares and early waking into the placid acceptance of Alan's death and what they had done with him as something in the past, and now to – what? She could not really believe that Alan had left the tank?

Sue replaced the slabs. It was all silliness. She could not make sure that Alan was still there without fishing for him. *"Hope to see you soon."* It was silliness, whatever it was, silliness. Jan was right; it was a piece of mischief to upset them by that girl at the Manor whom they had never met. The Christmas card had been worrying, really worrying for a while, but this was over the top; one could not give it importance. She marched over the lawn, her wellies squelching, militant in her soggy duffel coat. She would have to change before going back to the shop unless (the day being what it was, and passing trade unlikely) she did not bother to return at all. There was a fire in the living-room. She could sit on the floor on a waterproof sheet, and do finger-painting with Butch.

Even if the weather had been clear, the shrubbery is hidden from the woods by the house and dairy. Even if a watcher were to shift along the edge of the woods to the south in order to extend the field of vision, there is a line of hedge and the steep fall of the rockery to hide the shrubbery from observation. And rain itself is a discouragement to watching, insinuating itself inside the collar of an anorak and misting the lenses of binoculars. Nobody but Janet and Butch saw Susan moving the slabs from the septic tank.

*
149

The girls did not write to tell Bob about the postcard either, but this time it was out of consideration for his feelings and for those of Alan's parents. *"Hope to see you soon,"* and an Oxford postmark. It would do no good to get them all steamed up with hope, setting them off on a false trail, since the girls knew well enough that Alan was dead, and the postcard must be some kind of joke.

If it was a joke. Janet, still not at all sure that it was, did not see what else it could be. She was deeply troubled and perplexed, but survived it as most people do by going on from day to day.

It may be worth reminding ourselves at this point in the story how much the people principally concerned actually knew. The girls knew that Alan was dead, had never completed his journey to London, but had decomposed in the septic tank. They knew that Alan had told Bob about his meeting with Janet at the Inland Waterways Rally, and that he had brought Bob to see them, so that Bob must know of Alan's wish to keep Jan as a friend. Therefore, when Alan had disappeared, Bob had come to the village in search of him, following one of what must be a number of possible lines of investigation. They knew that Susan's evasiveness at the Flower Show had aroused unspecified suspicions in Bob, and that he had communicated these suspicions to Duncan, the local policeman, but they did not know of the circumstances of that meeting, which had allowed Bob to blackmail Duncan, first into making an inquiry, and then to reporting the result of it to Bob himself. They knew that Janet had explained Susan's evasiveness to Duncan, and assumed that he had been satisfied with that explanation, since after six months they had heard no more of the matter from him or any policeman. They did not know that Duncan had made his report to Bob, but did know, as all the village knew, that Duncan was having his end away with Fiona, daughter of the Manor, and therefore suspected that he might have told her what Janet had told him.

Duncan knew no more than has already been stated. Mrs Marshall knew all that the girls knew.

Bob knew that Alan had met Janet at Sykehouse, been much taken with her, and wished to keep her as a friend. He also now knew that Alan was Butch's father, but had no reason to believe that Alan knew, since, if Alan had, he would almost certainly have spoken of it to Bob, his closest friend and counsellor, and would also have been taking an active interest in Butch's welfare, even to the neglect of early musical instruments. Bob knew that Alan had told his parents that he was making a visit to London. Therefore it had to be assumed that he might have gone there, and Bob had made enquiries in London, and shown Alan's photograph, and had found no trace of him, but London is a large city in which many folk in transit float and some may sink without remark. Bob knew of no reason why Alan should lie to his parents about the London trip, but he knew that Alan had no friends in London unless he had secretly made some in the week before he left, and that Alan was a responsible business partner, unlikely to leave Bob in the lurch and even less likely to drop out of touch with the few close human contacts he had made in life so far. Therefore Bob wondered about that London trip, but he could not know that Alan had invented it as an excuse to visit the girls, that he had arrived without warning, discovered then that he had a son, been killed by Susan, and that now what was left of him was in the septic tank. Bob could not know this. Because we, who have read so far, do know it, we may be tempted to credit Bob with our own knowledge, but he could not know, could not even guess at it; he had no evidence for such a guess. His speculations went in many directions, particularly at night, particularly during the lonely hours, and since Alan had now been away a year with nothing heard from or of him, most of those speculations did include death in many of the various ways in which it may come.

Meanwhile Susan began to have nightmares again. Her nightmares also included death in various ways, some-

times for Jan, more often for Butch; they included various
sorts of punishment for herself, and mostly they included
Alan, already dead but by no means in a state of rest or
peace. Since she had forgotten what Alan looked like, the
Alan of her nightmares did not have a face.

"Hope to see you soon." Alan came for Butch early in May,
not at night but on a sunny Spring afternoon.

Jan was in the village, looking after the shop. Susan
and Butch were in the conservatory, transferring tomato
plants from the little peat pots in which they had started
as seed to the ten-inch clay pots in which they would
flourish and produce fruit. There had been some notion
that Butch might take a nap and allow Susan to pot on
the tomatoes by herself, but Butch had not been in the
napping mood that day. She had left him in his cot
upstairs after soothing conversation and with a lullaby by
Brahms at a low level on the cassette-player while she
scrubbed out the clay pots in the garden pool, but the
sounds of Butch's discontent could be heard even in the
garden, so she had fetched him down to the conservatory
with the warning that all this commotion and naplessness
was bound to lead to an early bedtime.

He was really no trouble. He sat on the floor of the
conservatory on newspaper, and pushed about the pile
of peat-based compost with which Susan was filling the
pots. Pushing it about did the compost no harm, and the
compost would do Butch no harm, as long as he did not
try to eat it. The afternoon sun warmed the conservatory,
drawing out the pleasing aromas of peat and tomato
foliage. They would have tea when the job was done, and
then they might see again about a nap.

Bullocks were looking over the fence at the bottom of
the garden. The fields on either side of the house were
used for pasture, being considered too steep for cultivation, although the ridges of the old medieval open-field
system remained to show that these fields had been under

152

cultivation in less affluent times. Bullocks grazed the fields in the spring and early summer, to be followed by sheep. The bullocks, once fattened, were sent to Banbury market, and so to slaughter and eventual incorporation into the beef mountain of the European Economic Community; the sheep, it was said in the village, were exported to the Gulf States where their throats were ritually slit and their eyes eaten by oil-millionaires in *couscous*. Now it was bullocks, a group of six from the herd. They had the habit of coming to the fence, resting their heads on the top rail, and looking longingly at the lushness of the garden. Every year it would be the same. The girls never encouraged them with grass-clippings or prunings; all that kind of thing was composted, not wasted on other people's bullocks. Yet every year the bullocks of the neighbouring fields ignored the nourishing nettles and clumps of thistles of that ill-kept pasture to yearn after tulips, cowslips, polyanthus and primula. The hedge which bordered the vegetable garden had had to be reinforced with barbed wire and heavy-duty metal mesh. Great damage had been done in the past to blackcurrant bushes, and a previous plum planted too close to the hedge had been almost entirely eaten. Susan had wished to speak sternly to Mr Heavitree about the destruction of the plum, but had been dissuaded by Janet, who had reminded her that the girls relied upon the good will of the farmers on either side, who could never have expected the derelict farmhouse and yard set amongst their fields to be so transformed.

Anyway, here they were again, the bullocks, most of the herd dotted about the field, and this small group looking over the hedge. Susan had pointed them out to Butch – 'Look, Butch! Bullocks!'—but one could not be sure what Butch actually took in at this distance. He could certainly see them, and if they succeeded in catching his attention might point them out or wave at them, but to what extent did he know that they were beings different in kind from the crab-apple or the climbing rose? 'Bullocks!' Susan said. 'You never need to be frightened of

153

them, Butchles. They always run away if you're firm.'
Susan herself was a little frightened of the bullocks, and
unconvinced that they would always run away. She
avoided going for a walk in any field in which bullocks
were grazing, unless accompanied.

The telephone rang. It had rung several times already
that day, and the connection had been broken when she
had picked it up. There was something, she vaguely
remembered, called a trip-fault; perhaps she ought to call
the telephone engineer. However, on two occasions that
day there actually had been someone at the other end,
once Jan from the shop, once Edna about taking extra milk
because there was over-production amongst the goats, so
the fault must be intermittent. Nevertheless she
considered not answering. The telephone stopped
ringing. Immediately Susan felt both justified and guilty.
It began to ring again. 'Okay, Butch,' she said, 'off we go
again,' picked him up (since he should not be left alone
anywhere as perilous as the conservatory), and carried
him into the kitchen. This time the caller was not a trip-
fault, but some person wishing to sell her insurance, or a
pension scheme, or some such. Susan did not understand
it, particularly since the man began by saying that he was
conducting an in-depth survey of selected respondents,
and went on to insurance from that. Janet usually handled
such matters. The conversation was confused, and
rendered more so by Butch's persistent attempts to pull
the telephone wire out of the junction box.

She returned from the telephone to find bullocks in the
garden. 'Oh God!' she said. 'Oh God!' They would do
such damage; she must get them out. One of them was
already cropping the heather-bed; the other five stood
uncertainly on the lawn. The gate in the fence was open;
the latch must have come loose. Susan had always known
they could not trust that gate; it was not needed; it had
been a mistake to put it in. The group of five bullocks on
the lawn began to move forward, still a little puzzled by
the garden, unable to decide which of all its goodies to
sample first. Now one was trying the mimulus in the

154

stream, one had turned aside to dogwood, and one, dear God! was advancing purposefully towards the weeping pear. Could bullocks climb steps? If so, there were the bee-hives, which fortunately had never been moved back to their old position at the bottom of the garden by the shrubbery, or they would already have been knocked over, and the bullocks, maddened by the stings of enraged bees, would be running about committing hardly-to-be-imagined atrocities both on the garden and themselves.

'Butch! In!' She grabbed him, ran with him into the living-room, and plopped him into his play-pen. Butch did not care for this incarceration, and set up a shout, but she had no time to soothe him. There was no knowing what the bullocks might do, or how they could be got out if once they became dispersed. She herself must be careful not to disperse them. She had seen programmes on tele-vision in which shepherds with collie dogs drove sheep into pens. Why had she and Jan never bought a dog? Shut up, Butch, and calm down, Susan. She would not be able to control the bullocks unless she first controlled herself. Everything must be done with authority. Susan breathed deeply twice, drew herself up like a matador, left the conservatory, and walked down the steps from the top to the bottom lawn. From behind her in the house she could hear Butch still shouting. She opened her arms, and held them wide. She was the Angel Gabriel announcing the coming of Christ to the Virgin Mary. She stared at the bullocks. The one at the heather-bed had shifted his attention to cowslips, but the others lifted their heads and stared back at her. Yes, one branch of the weeping pear had been shredded. It was not important; she had done as much herself with the lawn-mower. She looked at the five bullocks, and they looked at her. She had their attention; now she must exert authority. 'Shoo!' Susan said.

The leading bullock lowered its head. It had vestigial horns, which it was pointing at her. The other four moved up a little behind it, still staring at her. Susan thanked

God silently for creating cowslips, but there were still five bullocks to be faced. They were not bulls; they were not in any way dangerous; they had been castrated; they would back away if she moved towards them. The one which had lowered its head now tossed its head, and stamped one foot on the lawn. Bullocks did not charge human beings; they never charged; one only thought they might. No more procrastination, Sue must do it; she must make her move. She pushed one leg in front of the other. It had obeyed her, which proved she had control. Since her arms were shaking, it seemed wiser to lower them to her sides. She moved the other leg in front of the first. The five bullocks facing her did not move at all in any direction, but the one at the heather-bed turned its head, and seemed as if it would come upon her by the flank.

If she ran, they would run after her. She must not run. Nor must she allow them to disperse and wreck the garden. She had moved forward two steps, and must continue to do so. Where was authority? Somehow authority, craven creature, had wandered away, and left Susan rigid with fear. Neverthless she moved. The leading bullock took a pace backwards, but only to bring him closer to his colleagues; they continued to watch her. Onwards. She had reached the weeping pear. The bullocks continued to take backwards steps; if they backed into the shrubbery, that could not be helped. She moved a little sideways as well as forwards to put herself into position for a clear drive towards the gate. If she were to trip on any of the larger plants of the water-garden, or on one of the waterfalls by way of which the stream was conducted out of the garden, why then, she supposed, the bullocks would be on her, gashing her with their vestigial horns and trampling her underfoot. Therefore she would not slip. Come back, authority! 'Shoo, you buggers!' Susan said, hoping that the words sounded more authoritative to the bullocks than they did to her. It worked. The leading bullock turned aside, and began to walk in front of her, the other four following, towards the open gate. Then Susan realised that the sixth bullock from the heather-bed had fallen in behind her. She could both feel and smell its breath.

Susan walked with the calmness of total fear between bullocks to the gate. It was not true that bullocks never charged; if you turned your back on them, they always charged. Her only hope must be that the one following her might believe that she was another bullock. The first five walked through the gate and into the field. Susan stepped aside. The sixth bullock followed his fellows. She closed the gate carefully, and shook it to make sure that the latch was secure. She did not see how it could have become unlatched; the latch did not seem to be loose at all. Nevertheless she and Jan would look at it together later when she had stopped shaking. At least Butch was no longer shouting. She had not noticed when he had stopped. She had better go back and see to him, in case he should be feeling rejected. She returned to the house, noticing that two of the bullocks had left cow-pats on the lawn, which would have to cleaned up since they would be too strong for the grass in their raw state.

Butch was not in his play-pen. Susan's sensibilities had been so numbed by her experience with the bullocks that this did not at first alarm her. He never had been able to get out of his play-pen, and it was assumed that he would not be able to do so for at least another year, but somehow he had done so, and would have to searched for. 'Butch!' He did know his name, and would come to it in walking games across the floor or patio. 'Butch!' He was nowhere in the living-room. Now alarm did begin to stir. The kitchen, in spite of all their precautions, still contained some objects which could be dangerous to an unaccompanied nearly-two-year-old. 'Butch?' But he was not in the kitchen. The front door was closed and so was the back door to the shed and downstairs loo. He had not been in the conservatory, or she would have seen him when he came in. 'Butch!' No, he was not in the conservatory. The stairs! She tried the gate put in to keep Butch from the stairs. It was loose. 'Butch! Butch!' But he had not fallen downstairs or he would still be there, lying

157

huddled at the bottom. She went up the stairs, two at a time. 'Butch?' He was not in either of the bedrooms. He was not in the attic or the bathroom. He was not on any landing. He was not in the house at all.

'Butch!' He was not in the garden, not in any of the gardens, his head not crushed like an egg against one of the stones in the rockery. And anyway the front door had been shut. 'Butch!' He was not in the dairy, not face down on quarry tiles where Alan had lain, and anyway all the doors of the house, including the door to the dairy, had been shut. 'Butch! Butch!' He was not among the bee-hives, puffy and pink from bee-stings, nor among the chicken-litter, or in any of the adjacent fields, crumpled amid mud and nettles. And anyway all the doors had been shut. Butch could not open doors yet; the handles were too high, the latches too stiff. Butch could not yet climb out of his cot or over the sides of his play-pen. And all the doors had been shut.

"Hope to see you soon." Now she realised; now she knew. Alan had not come for Butch by night, when the girls would have defied him, defied him dead or alive, fought him away with claws and crucifix, opposing the strength of their own love to whatever power he had acquired. He had not come in wind or rain or sent a fog ahead from the land of the undead to hide him. He had tricked Susan, coming by day and in sunlight when the undead do not usually stir. He had tricked her doubly, using Susan's own concern for the garden to distract her from what should have been her greatest concern, the safety of the child.

'Butch!' What good did it do to call when he could not hear? He could not have moved himself out of the reach of her intense search, yet there was no one living to move him. He was nowhere to be found, yet he could not have been taken nowhere; he must be somewhere. Do not search aimlessly, Susan; think where Alan himself would take his son, to be with him and stay with him forever. There was only one place.

The knowledge of what must have happened was like

158

something growing inside her brain, pushing outwards so that her head would split. She must get Janet, who would somehow make all right again, so that nothing had happened, and Susan could not be blamed. She ran to the telephone in the kitchen, dialled the number of the shop, but there was nothing, only silence; the line was dead. Earlier, during the conversation about insurance, Butch had tried to pull the cord away from the junction box, but she had prevented that. Now the end of the cord lay on the kitchen window-sill, a yard from the box.

Butch was gone. Alan had taken him. She could not reach Janet. Susan ran to the septic tank, screaming like a crazy woman, pushing through shrubs and tugging at the concrete slabs. 'Give him back! He's no good to you. He's alive and you're dead. Give him back!' There was no response, only the dark polluted water, into which she could not see. Susan was beyond fastidiousness, beyond revulsion; she had to know. She reached into the tank, plunging her arm in up to the shoulder, bringing her own face, her own mouth, down almost to the level of the liquid. 'Give him back!' Her hand at full stretch moved in the sludge and found something it could grasp. She pulled it up and out of the tank. It was a bone, probably a thigh-bone. Alan had not left the tank. He was still to be found there, if one searched for him.

Susan sat back on her haunches, and looked at the bone. She supposed that she had better wash, but there was so much to do. She dropped the bone back in the water, and replaced the slabs. She went back across the lawn, and up the rockery, and had reached the front gate before she remembered that Jan had the Transit van, so that she herself would have to walk to the village. She looked for a moment at her arm, where the short sleeve of her dress was wet and stained with slime. Then she set off across the fields, ignoring the bullocks who displayed no interest in her. All this, even what she did at the tank, particularly what she did at the tank, was observed by the watcher.

The walk to the village across the fields is only twenty

159

minutes. When Susan and Janet arrived back together in the van, and ran into the house, Butch was sitting in his play-pen, attempting to destroy the koala bear which had been his first birthday present on the morning, nearly a year before, when Susan had met the man on the white horse. The cord of the telephone was still resting on the sill, pulled away from the junction box, but, as Susan herself admitted, Butch had been trying to pull it away during the whole of the insurance conversation, when her concentration had been, for part of the time, distracted.

12

AN UNFORTUNATE ACCIDENT

This is not a mystery story. You know well enough by
now that the watcher was Bob. He had sent the card at
Christmas to see whether the girls would find a way to
let him know that they had received it. If they had done
so, he would have felt able, as the police say, to eliminate
them from his enquiries. That they had not done so indicated either that they were extremely selfish and inconsid-
erate, which he doubted, or that they had something to
hide. Then they had not told anyone about the postcard
from Oxford either – "*Hope to see you soon*", when they
knew of his own anxiety, and Alan's parents', and that
there was a police investigation, however lax; they had
not even told Duncan. He had felt justified in going
further, and now he knew.

The question for Bob was what to do with the knowledge now he had it. He found himself strangely reluctant
to inform the police. He tried to account for his reluctance
by telling himself that the police would only think he was
a nutter, his whole story invented to annoy the girls, but
the reasoning would not hold. He could tell Duncan, who
already knew a part of the story. He could go himself to
the septic tank by night in darkness and rain while the
girls were sleeping, grope for a bone as he had seen Susan
do, and produce it in evidence. Presented with such a
positive accusation, the police would be bound, however
apologetically, to investigate the septic tank, and then they
would find what they would find. Might they, however,

choose to believe that Bob himself had murdered Alan, and placed his bones in the septic tank to incriminate the girls? No, that would not do. There would be forensic evidence to confirm how and where Alan had decomposed. The girls would not escape. They would be for it.

Bob would not even need to make the accusation in person; he could write an anonymous letter. The question for Bob was why he did not do so, and why, when he had already found what he had come to seek, he still continued to keep a watch on the girls.

The question for Janet was whether Susan was going mad. It had come on her so suddenly; it had come with the postcard. There had been the business of the bullocks; that was upsetting, since Susan was known to be afraid of bullocks, but it could hardly account for delusions on such a scale. All the evidence seemed to be that Butch had never left his play-pen. There was nothing whatever, no scratch or graze on his body, no stains of grass or mud on his dungarees, to indicate that he had been taken from the house for half an hour; certainly there was no slime from the septic tank. Children were sometimes stolen, usually by discontented adolescent girls or by women who had themselves lost a child, but not borrowed for half an hour, and put back in exactly the same place with no indication that they had been away. As for the telephone cord, Susan admitted that Butch had been pulling at it, and admitted further, when gently pressed, that if Alan's ghost had indeed returned, it would not have needed to tear out the telephone, or been able physically to do it. Butch himself would have been the best witness to what had happened, but unfortunately he could not yet speak a language the girls could understand.

Now Susan spoke of selling up, leaving the house and garden, giving up the shop, and settling somewhere else with Butch, although she knew well enough on the rational level that this was something the girls must never do, since only by remaining where they were could they ensure that the septic tank was never emptied. The question for Janet was how to get Susan to a doctor, yet how,

162

if Susan were induced to go, she could be prevented from saying too much.

The question for Susan was how to protect Butch. She would have left the house and run away with him, as far as they could, but Jan would not allow it. Jan did not believe what had happened. That was of no consequence; Susan herself, if she had been told about it instead of experiencing it, might have found it difficult to believe. What was important was that Alan had taken Butch once, and might again, and must be prevented. They must never leave Butch, even for a second. She insisted on having his cot moved into their bedroom, and was humoured. She also insisted that Butch must wear a crucifix at all times, and that the house should be hung with garlic. It was easy enough to buy a crucifix from an antique shop, but Butch took against it; perhaps he found it scratchy. Whatever the reason, he kept pulling it off. The girls shouted at each other in the kitchen. Jan, who was never angry, became red in the face, and Susan wept. In the end they were reconciled by the compromise of having the crucifix always in the pocket of Butch's dungarees, and hung up like a mobile on his cot at night, but the row was damaging.

As for the garlic, it had not yet come into season, and the previous year's supply was almost exhausted; there was not enough left to hang at every door and window, and more had to be bought from a greengrocer. This bought garlic was poor stuff, dried up and gone over, and its presence puzzled Mrs Marshall when she came up to clean on Wednesday. Janet told her that Susan had been reading an article about the beneficial effects of garlic, how just having it about the place cleared the lungs of phlegm and kept away insect pests, notably whitefly. It was a fad, Janet said; it would not last; none of Susan's fads lasted; meanwhile they must put up with it.

So Wednesday passed, and Thursday, with no questions answered. Just as much as Susan's, Bob's mind became the playground of lurid ideas. Why should Alan be the only one? How many young men so far, Bob wondered, had been murdered and dropped into the septic tank? He himself had met Susan only twice, Jan not at all, and although Alan's description of Jan had been of someone essentially kind, commonsensical and a good companion, Alan might have been mistaken or even deliberately deceived by someone assuming the kind of personality most calculated to meet his emotional needs. Might have been? – must have been; look what had happened to him. Perhaps the personality was not assumed, but multiple; Bob had heard of such cases, one moment the direct gaze and ready sympathy, the next a monster, ravening for blood. He looked back through a long experience of Craft Fairs, and saw on the periphery of every memory a psychopathic killer concealed amongst the smocks and clogs and home-made fudge. They would have sent Alan a message during the week Bob had been away. 'Come and see us. Don't tell anyone.' And so it had been done, to him as to the others, a long line of vulnerable young men, needing attention, needing friends, like pet lambs running to the abattoir. How many Alans in the septic tank, and murdered in what manner? Sex first, perhaps with both, and then the knife? cleaver? wire? poison? Trussed up and battered to death? carved in strips? eaten?

Question and speculation, horrible imaginings! so they went. Bob's mind did not require the stimulus of late-night television and tales of the undead; it was nourished by reality, by what could be read any day in the newspapers or heard on the radio. No horror can be invented by a writer of fiction which has not already happened. Who could invent the Holocaust, the Vietnam War, Laos, Idi Amin, the death squads of Argentina and San Salvador, the Fifth Brigade of President Mugabe and the prison camps of Iran where political prisoners are drained of blood to provide transfusions for fifteen-year-old soldiers? Literature follows and feeds on history; it does not lead.

But although there were precedents even for the worst of what Bob could imagine, and the imaginings them-

164

selves were out of his control and gave him grief, they did not hold up against logic. If the girls had sent such a message, how could they have known that Bob would be away when Alan received it? 'Don't tell anyone', but he would always tell Bob; experienced murderers would not have run such a risk. And Butch! However long a line of victims Bob's imagination might present to him, there was only one Butch. Alan must, therefore, have been special; there was no line of victims unless there had been a child by each, in which case where were the other children? That Alan was dead was certain, but Susan had not behaved like someone accustomed to murder – if it was murder. Bob knew where Alan had been put, but not what had been done to him. He could not even be sure that Janet knew; it might have been done while she was away or ill. He had observed that it did not seem to matter to the girls which of them looked after Butch as long as one of them was always with him. Susan had been on her own with him during the afternoon on which Bob had released the bullocks and borrowed Butch, otherwise he would not have been able to do it. Was it possible that Alan had arrived on that day in March to find only Susan in the house with Butch, that somehow and for some unknown reason she had killed him and disposed of the body, and told Jan nothing about it? Come to that, why had Bob himself chosen Susan and not Jan for his experiment? Was it because he secretly wanted Jan to be innocent or because he had decided that Susan was the one more likely to crack?

Once questions begin, there is no end to them. The whole matter required a great deal more thought. Bob had been staying in a bed-and-breakfast at Stratford, and travelling to his observation post by rented bicycle, so as not to have to leave his car at the top where it might be noticed. Now that the tourist season had begun, the rents of both had risen and were beginning to make a hole in his denuded savings. He decided to go back up north for a while, and brood. There were kits requiring assembly; he had orders to fill. He would return with a tent in better weather. The girls would not go away, nor would the evidence. All could be left to simmer.

Sometimes Susan talked of moving Alan from the septic tank. They would make a concrete plinth for the compost heap, and put him under it, or even in it. Or they would take the bones in a black plastic bag to some public Refuse Tip, not local but at a distance. They would drive into Lancashire or even to the border of Scotland, and look in the telephone book for a suitable tip. They would not be noticed among all the other people bringing old mattresses and unrepairable lawn-mowers for disposal; one dumps one's own rubbish unsupervised. The people in charge of the tips never looked inside black plastic bags but simply pushed them into great heaps with a bulldozer and grassed them over. It would be like a burial for Alan.

She began to spend hours sitting in the conservatory, staring at the shrubbery. She would not leave the house, even to take a turn at looking after the shop. She said that Jan should go, and take Butch with her. He would be safe in the shop. Susan would remain in the house in case Alan should return. She would know what to do. There was the shotgun (though one could hardly expect it to fire silver bullets even if she had any), and she kept an axe behind the door of the shed. What with the axe and the garlic, Alan would not know what hit him. She did not wish Jan to stay in the house to face Alan, if he were to come. He was Susan's responsibility; if she had not killed him, they would not be in this trouble. Anyway there was always plenty to do in the house and garden; she would not be idle.

Nevertheless Susan was mostly idle during these later days of May. She did the washing-up and made the beds, and spent the rest of the time in the conservatory. At night, as never before except during the days of the Black Panther, all the doors were locked.

Janet went to the Public Library, and borrowed every-

166

thing she could find, which was not much, on the subject of schizophrenia. She did not take these books home, but read them in the shop between serving passing trade and keeping an eye on Butch. In some ways Susan's behaviour was not as alarming as it had been in the period before Crete, when she had watered everything and was always in tears, but depression is known to pass, whereas schizophrenia may require lifelong medication. At present, Susan was getting no medication at all, and Janet became convinced that it would only be a matter of time before she began hearing voices and neglected to wash. She must see somebody. Dr Barnes had been both sympathetic and discreet in the matter of Janet's own pregnancy, and would anyway be bound by the Hippocratic oath, and yet . . . and yet, confronted by an act which was not murder, but might be considered so, where would Dr Barnes decide that her duty lay? It would not be fair to Dr Barnes to place such a weight on her discretion. Janet reminded herself that once she had had her own access to psychiatric help. It had been ten years since she had left the Probation Service, and she had not kept in touch with any of her Oxford collagues, but someone must still be there, to remember her and point her in the right direction. Oxford was only an hour away, but the paths of Oxford people and the village people never crossed. A sophisticated Oxford psychiatrist, who had seen everything and was surprised by nothing, might even decide that a belief that one had killed a young man was all part of the schizophrenic syndrome, and if she did, Janet would not undeceive her.

Of course she could not get Susan to anyone qualified to help her unless Susan would agree to go. Since Susan did not believe herself to schizophrenic, and anyway the subject was never discussed, this constituted a problem.

In Yorkshire meanwhile, Bob seriously considered sending the anonymous letter. It would save so much trouble and embarrassment to let the police take over, but it would be anti-climactic after he had come so far on his own. Bob wanted justice to be done, yet he did not wish to be the instrument of justice, nor was he sure what justice was in this case. Looking for Alan, at first despairingly because he had decided he must, then with an increasing conviction of success, had given him a purpose. He had stood at the edge of the woods, holding Butch in his arms, and watched Susan run screaming to the septic tank, and had felt triumph, had felt justified, but already the feeling of justification had become obscured, the triumph a little shabby. He had told himself that his quest was unfinished; he must go on; he did not yet know absolutely what had happened. He had promised himself that he would return with a tent, but what action was he then to take? His purpose demanded confrontation, yet he shrank from it. An anonymous letter would be simpler; the thing would be over; he would no longer be involved. But he did not send it.

He brought off a coup, long wished for, by persuading the local College of Adult Education to set up a course of evening classes on Early Music, which he would teach. The remuneration would not be much, but he should be able to sell instruments to his students. He would encourage them to form a consort. The course was to begin in the autumn, but it was all ashes. He missed Alan. Making up the kits was a job for two. Bob had many friends, but somehow he neglected to see them. He was lonely. Alone in the bed-and-breakfast in Stratford, watching alone in the woods, he had not been lonely.

Bob had opened the gate in the fence and driven the bullocks into the garden while Susan had been answering the telephone. He had entered the house by the front door, to find Butch shouting in his play-pen, enraged at being abandoned. He had lifted Butch out of the pen, and at once Butch had stopped shouting; he enjoyed attention, and had no distrust of adults, since he knew so few, and all friendly. Bob had said, 'Here we go to market!' and 'Joggitty, joggitty, jog!' as they had made the journey to the woods, and the two of them had watched Susan disposing of the bullocks, Susan searching for Butch, Susan at the septic tank, and finally Susan walking across fields down to the village. Butch had pulled at leaves, and had reached up to Bob's beard, and explored it intimately, had put one finger up Bob's nostril, and tugged at Bob's ear. They had conversed quietly together on matters of no great moment, and when Susan had gone Bob had brought Butch back again, put him in the pen, rubbed the side of his cheek, said, 'See you, then!' and been allowed to leave without protest while Butch rediscovered the Koala bear.

Alan would have been pleased about the adult education classes; they had discussed the possibility together. He would not have been qualified to teach, but he would have helped with the equipment. Bob knew that he ought to look for another partner, but he could no more begin to do so than he could write the anonymous letter.

Bob hitch-hiked south with a tent. He had decided not to bring the car because there would be nowhere to leave it safely. Very soon he made the discovery that hitch-hiking is for the young. His rucksack had lain unused in a cupboard for some years, and no longer seemed to fit his back. The tent, however compactly he might contrive to pack it, still made a bulky roll to be strapped to the top of the rucksack, and bounced up and down as he walked, abrading the back of his neck. He walked through several miles of the outskirts of Doncaster in this fashion, since his attempt to catch a bus was thwarted by his becoming stuck in the door. Then he stood for two hours at the side of the road waiting for a ride that would take him five miles to the motorway, while younger hitch-hikers in less advantageous positions were picked up within minutes. Motorists, as a general rule, even the kindest of them, do not choose to give lifts to fat hairy hitch-hikers in their thirties, whose shirts are already soaked with sweat, and who are burdened with rucksacks and bedding rolls almost as large as themselves.

He waited again on the slip-road to the motorway, until a lorry-driver took pity on him, and gave him a lift to the junction for Daventry. The lorry-driver was from the north-east, his accent almost incomprehensible and made more so by the roar of the ill-maintained engine and the rush of wind through the windows wound down because of the heat. Though pity had moved him to stop, yet he required a return in the way of conversation, which would not only relieve the tedium of the journey, but allow him to express resentments and anxieties which had perhaps found no other outlet. Bob was never quite sure at any time what they were talking about. It might have been snooker; it might have been the fortunes of some Geordie football team in danger of relegation; it might have been the insatiable sexual demands of the driver's wife, the malevolence of his employers, or the iniquity of having to carry a tachograph in the cab, or it might have been all of these in combination. Bob sat and sweated in the cab, crowded by his rucksack, and tried to make replies which were sympathetic without being specific. It was already evening by the time they reached Junction 18.

Darkness would not fall until ten p.m. The distance still to cover was less than forty miles, but across country and with a choice of several routes. Bob began on what he took to be the Oxford road, from which he would branch west, but the hitch-hiker who waits long will accept any lift. He veered first towards Leamington, then lost his way among minor roads, and spent the night in a dry ditch using the rolled-up tent as a pillow. He woke with the dawn, his belly empty, his mouth fetid, his hair and beard sticky with the seeds of goose-grass, and set out to walk the rest of his journey.

He washed and tidied himself at a bus-station, drank tea and breakfasted off a chocolate biscuit and one of those elderly sausage rolls which are kept under glass like some national treasure. He began to feel a sense of achievement. There were no buses going his way that day, but a bus to Warwick would shorten his journey by two miles. He bought staples in Warwick – bread, apples, beer, processed cheese and one of those tins of pilchards which open by pulling at a ring-top. He set out to walk again, and reached the woods by early afternoon. There, deliberately, with due attention to the instructions provided, he erected the tent; it presented no challenge to a man who could build a spinet from a kit. Bob would make no fires, create no litter, would defecate at a distance and bury the spoil; he had brought a trowel. He would be a model camper, and no one would know of his presence. Meanwhile he must catch up on sleep; he had plans for the night. He stripped to his underclothes, lay down inside the tent, and fell asleep almost immediately.

He was awakened by a gamekeeper. 'I don't know what you think you're doing here.'

'Sorry?'

'You're out of line, my friend; you're altogether out of line.' The gamekeeper had at his heels a dog of some indeterminate breed. It had already pissed on the tent, and was now looking up at its master as if for further instructions. The gamekeeper wore a tweed cap and knickerbockers, but his accent was urban Birmingham, and his glasses glinted with that cold light which is found only in Town Halls and among the upper echelons of the BBC. 'I shouldn't have to tell you this is private property. You're committing a nuisance.'

Bob had a hazy recollection of having read in some Ramblers' Guide that there could be no trespass without damage. He groped for his trousers, and pulled them on, still seated. 'What nuisance?'

'Being here.'

'That's hardly a nuisance.'

'It is to me. It's a nuisance having to move you on, when I should be having my tea at home. We don't get paid overtime on this job, you know. It's a twenty-four-hour-employment with no perks, whatever the public may imagine. So we'll have you packing up and moving on, if you don't mind, before I lose my temper.'

'I'm doing no damage.'

'Are you trying to teach me the law?'

'I just said I'm doing no damage.'

'It's erroneous, is that, in more than one respect. First, it's bad law. It's not up to me to prove you're doing any damage. I merely have to instruct you that you are on private property, and should you refuse to leave, either inform the authorities or make a citizen's arrest.' The gamekeeper's knickerbockers were kept up by a wide leather belt to which, Bob noticed, a knife was attached in a sheath, and the man's hand tapped this sheath as he spoke. 'Secondly, you cannot move in these woods, no member of the public can, without committing ecological malfeasance. Touch but a leaf, my friend, bend but a twig, and the whole course of Nature may be perverted. So start making a move, is what I'm telling you.'

'Should you be carrying a knife? It's an offensive weapon, isn't it?'

'Used for disembowelling rabbits. Sometimes fed to the dog, sometimes made into rabbit pie, in which case the dog gets only the entrails. Now, I've told you to move on. I must ask you formally if you are refusing to do so.'

'Couldn't I stay the night, and move on in the morning? I'm not doing any harm.'

The gamekeeper's watch was large, with a digital display and a strap of metal mesh. Bob had seen such watches. They were designed to perform many functions, amongst them those of a calculator. The watch now began to sound an alarm, which the gamekeeper switched off. 'That is to remind me that my tea will be ready. By now, it may be in the oven, drying up under a plate. I'm warning you; I shall return to my cottage, have tea, watch the news on t.v., and come back here in two hours' time precisely. If you have not left these woods, I shall arrest you and give you in charge. I hope that is clear. Good dog! Come follow!'

He strode off without a backward glance, the dog following. Twigs bent, and brambles snagged his knickerbockers. Leaf mould was crunched underfoot. Gloomily Bob began to pack up the tent. He had seen a farmhouse b-and-b on his way, but that had been three miles back,

172

and some farmhouses these days had found their way into the Good Food Guide, and were expensive.

Wednesday morning. Bob walked into Stratford to buy a fishing net. Mrs Marshall came up from the village to clean, and to create her flower arrangements.

'He's back then, as I hear.'

'Who's back?'

'Fat man at the Flower Show. Set up a tent in the woods. Sleeping in his undies, great hairy object!'

Janet closed the kitchen door. Susan was at the other end of the house in the conservatory, pollinating tomatoes with a paintbrush. 'He's in the woods?'

'You'd better be getting down to the shop, day like this. Good day for trading.'

'What's he doing in the woods?'

'Gone now. Bert Armitrage sent him packing. Frighten the pheasants. Private property. Bert Armitrage, he knows his law. Teaches Judo Tuesday evenings at the Village Hall. Beryl Gaines signed up for it, him being a widower, but he put her neck out in the demonstration. "You bugger off," he says, "before you provoke me to a citizen's arrest." Hairy object packed his tent and left.'

'Where is he now?'

'Soryton Farm, bed and breakfast.'

'He'll be back, then.'

Mrs Marshall, tall as a grenadier, kept herself in fighting trim. 'You be off down the shop, my dear. Take Butch with you. Don't fear for Susan. I'm not leaving this house until you get back. He's got no transport, as I hear; it's Shanks's pony. Let him come, asking questions; I'll see to him. Better me than you; catch him wrong-footed. Give him something he don't expect, my dear; I've been obstreperous in my day. Run him off his feet; that's the way with fatties. Bloody heart attack; I'll harry the bugger.' Mrs Marshall had a small portable black-and-white television set in her caravan, worked by a car

173

battery, and watched Wimbledon assiduously. 'Wrong-footed, my dear. Let him come, I'll give him passing shots, I'll give him cross-court returns, I'll give him a volley to his guts, my dear; you trust me.' She took a large can of Trafficwax from the cupboard under the sink, and prepared to assault the electric floor-polisher. 'Bloody object!'

Bob did not come that day, though Mrs Marshall remained beyond her time, well prepared to demolish him with aces. He came by night. Either he had been stung by ants during his sleep in the dry ditch, or he had developed an allergy to goose-grass; for whatever reason, his skin was now disfigured with raised red bumps which itched infuriatingly. His feet were blistered, and one of the blisters had burst and become raw, and although he had covered it with an antiseptic dressing he feared infection. Nothing had gone right with Bob since he had begun his journey south. Consequently his judgment was impaired and his imagination inflamed. He would have proof in his hand, and he would confront the girls with it. They would cower and break, and he would force the truth from them, every scrap, no messing. Then he would decide what to do.

That is why he had bought the fishing net. It had strong green mesh and was large enough to take a trout; the shaft was of stainless steel, and extensible. It was far too good for his purpose, and cost more than he could afford, but it was what the shop had. Bob told himself that it was worth paying for certainty. The aggravation and expense would soon be over. One bold stroke would make an end.

What idiocy! Susan these days slept always on the edge of waking. She could hear the click of the latch of the gate, however carefully opened and refastened. She could hear one piece of gravel kicked against another on the drive and the dry rustle of yucca and lavender, however gently negotiated, at the top of the rockery. She knew that Alan was abroad. Janet had not told her about Bob's recent attempt to take up residence in the woods, but Susan would have discounted it anyway. She listened only for one visitor.

Bob had thought that he could easily find his way about the garden. It was not large, and he had all night. He had not appreciated the extent to which the girls masked unsightly straight lines with overgrowths of ground cover, clumps of bergamot, mimulus and bugle, lady's mantle and astilbe. He was totally unprepared for the potentilla in the rockery or for the lemon thyme which covered the steps going down towards the pool. He blundered into euonymus, pushed through giant cowslips, caught his fishing net in the weeping pear, stepped into the pool itself, floundered in mud and almost fell full tilt. However, he was in the bottom garden by this time, and the windows of the girls' bedroom did not overlook it. He would be safe enough if he continued to go cautiously. He entered the shrubbery and felt for the first time the sharp spines of berberis. Once more his fishing net became snagged. He struggled, as quietly as he could, with hostile vegetation in the darkness.

Sue slid sideways on the bed until she reached the edge, and listened to Jan's breathing and to Butch. Nothing out of the ordinary. She eased herself off the bed, and went on tiptoe to the bathroom. She took her old dressing-gown of terry towelling from the hook, and pulled it round her. Back to the top of the stairs. Listen again. Nothing. Downstairs slowly. She knew which stair always creaked, and avoided it. She was at the bottom of the stairs, and must now open the back door to the shed without waking anyone. Done. She took the axe from where she kept it by the door, and went through the shed to the conservatory. She could see that there was movement down in the shrubbery. Well, she had expected it.

Bob managed to get his fishing net free and himself through the berberis. Nettles stung his hands in the darkness. There was a smell of sewage. He found the concrete

175

slabs by falling over them. Now came the unpleasant part. He had brought a torch, but not used it so far. Now he would need it to inspect his catch. He moved one of the slabs aside and pushed back a second. He shone the torch onto the liquid in the tank. He thought of Alan's being plunged into this filth, and felt momentarily sick.

Susan could see a light in the shrubbery. That did not surprise her. She knew that the appearances of the undead were often accompanied by an unearthly light, usually greenish in colour. This light did not seem to be greenish, but it was obscured by shrubs, and might be more greenish closer to. She left the conservatory, and walked silently across the grass at the top of the lawn.

Bob dipped his fishing net into sewage until he could feel the bottom of the tank. He moved it about, scraping the bottom. The light of his torch did not penetrate this murky liquid. He must bring up what he could, ignoring whatever filth and shit might be down there, and keep on until he found what he was looking for. He pulled up the net, and shone the torch on what was in it. He had brought up a skull.

The axe was heavy, but Susan swung it easily as she walked. A sickle moon emerged momentarily from behind clouds, and illuminated the blade. It was a long-handled axe. With it she might be able to strike from the edge of the shrubbery, and take Alan by surprise. She supposed that she would have to chop him into a great many pieces in order to make sure that he never troubled them again, but the first blow would be the most important.

Bob switched off the torch. It had shown him what he had expected and feared to see, and now he would go on in darkness. He took the skull from the net. It was slimy and stinking, but that was only the sewage in the tank; the skull itself was clean bone; it was Alan's skull. Tears filled Bob's eyes. He clutched the skull in both hands, and bent his head over it. He could feel the grief inside him trying to get out, and bit his lip to hold it in. Let him howl, let him howl, what did it matter? The girls would know soon enough that he was in their garden. Oh, he would make his presence known!

The light in the shrubbery had gone, and the moon was again obscured. Susan stopped still. The darkness seemed thicker than it had been. Had Alan sensed her approach, and returned to the tank? Had he, as the undead were sometimes known to do, surrounded himself with a cloud of darkness from within which he would pounce? There was still a something in the shrubbery. She could see it shifting about. It was making noises, slobbery blubbery noises, there beside the septic tank. Let it blobber and slubber as much as it liked, it could not frighten Susan. She had Butch to protect, and Jan, and she would fight the thing on its own ground. She launched herself into the shrubbery, the axe held in both hands high over her head.

Bob turned, and saw through tears a pale shape come at him, the shape of a mad woman in a robe of terry towelling, holding an axe. He thought of Alfred Hitch-cock's *Psycho*, and screamed. There was an explosion, which seemed to come from somewhere nearer the house, and a flash of flame. The mad woman jerked and fell forwards; the axe toppled sideways out of her hands. Bob rolled away as it fell, and found himself half in and half out of the septic tank. From the direction of the house there came the sound of running, and a voice crying in the dark, 'Susan! Susan!'

She lay on the lawn, covered by blankets, while they waited for the ambulance. She seemed to be in some pain, but Janet had been told not to move her and not to give her aspirin or any painkiller, only warm tea against the shock. Susan had seemed disinclined to drink warm tea, and they had not pressed it on her. She was conscious, but seemed not to understand what had happened. It was all seeming with Susan; that was the trouble. They knew very little for sure except that the ambulance would

177

definitely come, and the men had understood the directions for finding the house, and would telephone from the box in the village if they became lost.

They had had to lift Susan out of the shrubbery; she could not be left entangled in berberis. Anyway that had been before Janet telephoned for the ambulance, so they had not yet received instructions. There seemed to be some trouble with Susan's back. She said she could not move her legs. They had carried her to the place where she now lay very tenderly and carefully, supporting her back as well as they could. She had not cried out at all when they carried her, not even moaned or whimpered, but there was blood on her mouth where she had bitten her lip against the pain. She was moaning a little now, but did not seem to know that she was doing so. Of course if she was in shock one could tell nothing about her back or legs or anywhere else.

'How long do you think it will take?'

'Could be half an hour. Longer if there isn't an ambulance ready.' What Jan most wanted to do was to get Sue into the van, and drive her straight to hospital, but she had agreed that it would be better to wait if there was even the slightest possibility of an injury to the back. The ambulance men would have diagnostic experience of a sort, and a stretcher and proper painkillers which they would know how to administer. As long as Sue was kept warm and comfortable, there was no danger in delay. Jan had been asked for very little in the way of an explanation. She supposed that all that would come later. Alan's skull had been put back in the tank.

'She didn't mean to kill him. She tried to revive him. Kiss of life, and that sort of thing. Ironic really.'

'I know.' Bob did not know; he had not even properly taken it in, but 'I know' seemed to be the right thing to say.

'He said something about having a son. How it changed a man. She thought he might want to come and live with us, or even take Butch away.'

'I know.' Sue made a small sharp sound of pain, and

178

Jan crouched down beside her to stroke her face. She longed to hold her, but dared not; it seemed unfair.

Bob said, 'He wouldn't have wanted to come and live with you. He did want friends, though. Friends of his own.'

'I know.'

Bob sat on the grass opposite Jan, with Sue between them. He touched Sue's cheek, and she did not flinch away. He was fat and hairy, and he squelched when he sat down because his clothing was still soaked, and he stank from the septic tank. He said, 'There was a man on television. Some arts programme. Famous American writer. Gore Something. He said there's no point in writing about victims, because they're not interesting. Only rich and powerful people are interesting. Then he went on about Greek tragedy; I couldn't follow all of it. Alan was a victim. Bound to be, I think, from birth. It seems a pity he's not a proper subject for literature. Victims are the only people one can like. This Gore Somebody said that even when you write about sex, it should be the mating of eagles. I still remember it. The mating of eagles.'

'It wasn't exactly that.'

'I know.'

'It's all been about Butch really, hasn't it? Having him seems to have caused a lot of trouble.'

'I'm not going to tell anyone. You have to stay together and look after him; there's no question. Imagine what it could do to him, all the publicity, having it hanging over him all his life. I couldn't possibly tell anyone.'

They could see the lights of the ambulance on the road above the cottage, first a glow among the trees, then the two beams of the headlights and then the vehicle itself with the blue of the warning light on top. Jan said, 'You'd better go in and keep out of sight. Get yourself cleaned up as well as you can. Then you can sit with Butch until I get back.'

13

THE GIRLS

Miss Burt had heard the latch of the gate and the sound of footsteps on the gravel drive. She had got up at once and gone to see what was up, leaving Miss Hallas with the toddler. Miss Hallas had become anxious, and followed her, taking the shotgun which was kept in case of rabbits in the vegetable garden. She had heard Miss Burt call out from the lower garden, had run towards the direction of the sound, and had seen indistinctly in the darkness that Miss Burt was struggling with some intruder, who seemed to be trying to drag her into the shrubbery, perhaps with the object of rape. She had panicked, and fired at the man's legs, and being totally unused to guns of any sort, had not allowed for the kick; the rabbits had always been Miss Burt's responsibility. Even Miss Burt was by no means an expert, and had bought cartridges of the wrong sort, Number One instead of Number Six, each filled with about eighty metal pellets about the size of ball-bearings, more suited to the shooting of wild geese than of rabbits; this may be the reason why so few rabbits had actually been shot on the property. At a range of just over fifteen yards the pellets formed a cluster about the size of a grapefruit, which struck Miss Burt in the middle of the back, causing a comminuted fracture of the thoracic vertebrae. In the confusion which followed, the intruder made good his escape. Police investigation confirmed that there had been a struggle of some sort at the edge of the shrubbery, and threads of what may have been a man's heavy-knit blue pullover and grey corduroy trousers were found caught on thorns. The man himself has never been found, nor can one be sure that he has committed any offence. Miss Hallas blames herself for the accident, no one else.

Of course it is particularly inconvenient to be confined to a wheelchair when one's house is halfway down a hill, a mile from the village over fields, three miles by road, but the girls are determined not to move. There are ramps everywhere, even a portable ramp in the back of the van, and a system of ropes and ratchets has been attached to the stairs so that Susan can pull herself up, and then proceed to bed by means of rings set in the wall. The downstairs w.c. has been greatly enlarged and converted to a bathroom, and the height of all the work-tops altered in the dairy. A man comes weekly from the village to do the gardening. Mrs Marshall, until her death, increased her visits from one a week to two to help with the housework and arrange flowers, and now her daughter-in-law has taken her place.

In the shop the wheelchair has its advantages. Susan is so very cheerful and gallant that passing trade is seduced by her gallantry into buying recklessly, as if contributing to famine relief. The mail-order flourishes. Janet's parents often visit, always bringing presents for Butch, who is now ten years old, and so do Susan's. Now that Susan is a cripple, it seems entirely appropriate to both sets of parents that Janet should look after her. The girls' elderflower wine continues to take First Prize at the Flower Show every year, and they entertain more than they used to do, giving buffet lunches in summer on the lawn to professional and business people in the district whom they have now taken the trouble to get to know.

Please do not presume to pity the girls. They continue to love each other, and it is possible to make love even when one of you has a broken back.

*

181

Time has passed. The extra-mural evening classes on Early Music have led to an attachment, first to the Music Department of one university, then another, sometimes abroad. I have spent academic years in South Dakota and in Western Australia. I no longer make up early musical instruments from kits to sell, no longer frequent Craft Fairs; I no longer hear from my ex-wife, Rachel, since she sold her Juice Bar in order to join an Organic Community near Rhyll; I no longer have a partner or any settled home. I visit the girls from time to time, spending perhaps as much as a week with them before I begin to feel surplus to their requirements. They are generous and hospitable friends. They are my only friends.

Oh, Alan, you were all I loved. You were my life, my heart, my present and my future. I loved you before I knew it, and when I knew it, I had already lost you. *Che faro senza lei? Che faro? Dove andro?*

What shall I do? Where shall I go?

But the child, the child is beautiful.